D1052937

My name is Callum Ormond.
I am fifteen
and I am a hunted fugitive . . .

CONSPIRACY 365

BOOK THREE: MARCH

To Hana, Jonathan, Liam and Lucy

First American Edition 2010
Kane Miller, A Division of EDC Publishing

Text copyright © Gabrielle Lord, 2010
Cover design copyright © Scholastic Australia, 2010
Illustrations copyright © Scholastic Australia, 2010
Back cover photo of boy's face © Scholastic Australia, 2010
Cover photo of boy peering © Scholastic Australia, 2010
Cover design by Natalie Winter
Illustrations by Rebecca Young
First published by Scholastic Australia Pty Limited in 2010
This edition published under licence from Scholastic Australia Pty Limited

Library of Congress Control Number: 2009934759

Printed and bound in the United States of America
1 2 3 4 5 6 7 8 9 10
ISBN: 978-1-935279-52-5

BOOK THREE: MARCH

GABRIELLE LORD

A DIVISION OF EDC PUBLISHING

PREVIOUSLY...

1 FEBRUARY
The oil had almost completely smothered me when the pump was suddenly turned off, and the tank cover was lifted. The mysterious Winter Frey had saved my life, but then she tells me that Vulkan Sligo, the guy who'd just left me to drown, is her guardian. How can I trust her?

3 FEBRUARY
Boges and I catch up at the St. Johns Street hideout. He helps me set up a blog so that I can try and tell my side of the story and clear my name.

9 FEBRUARY
Winter won't answer my calls so I decide to sneak back to the car lot to see if I can find her and get more information. I scan the place while hiding and am shocked when a guy sneaking around the yard, searching for parts, turns out to be a girl — Winter!

13 FEBRUARY

Desperate for a new break, I find my way back to the house I was held in when I was first abducted. From my position up in a tree, I take a quick snapshot of the woman inside — the fiery redhead who I'm sure is the one who interrogated me.

14 FEBRUARY

At the Central Station basketball courts I spot a guy that looks exactly like me! I try to approach him, but he runs away from me like he's seen a ghost.

16 FEBRUARY

Boges recognizes the redhead in my photo as being the well-known criminal lawyer Oriana de la Force. We have a close call with Rafe when he shows up with another guy at Burger Barn. Their conversation reveals that my uncle is signing his house over to my mum to try and help her cope.

19 FEBRUARY

My newest hideout, a storm water drain, gets flooded after a massive downpour, and I almost lose the drawings as I'm thrashed along, caught in the torrent.

20 FEBRUARY

A phone call to Eric Blair, one of my dad's colleagues, provides nothing — he's not in the office. But Winter finally calls, and we go to Memorial Park together to see the angel she'd been talking about. The moonlight through the cenotaph roof reveals a stained glass image of the Angel — a memorial to Piers Ormond — just as Dad had drawn him.

28 FEBRUARY

I'm clawed by a lion after sneaking into the zoo to try and make my meeting with Jennifer Smith. I flee the scene, but am tracked down later by Red Tank Top who chases me deep into the railway tunnels. After staging a fall on the tracks I jab him with one of my tranquilizers and run. The rumbling of an oncoming train forces me to go back and push his unconscious body off the tracks, but I slip awkwardly and find that my foot has become wedged somehow, and I'm now trapped in the train's deadly path . . .

1 MARCH

306 days to go . . .

Underground train line
Liberty Square

8:22 pm

There was rumbling and shaking all around as swirling, molten shapes rushed in on me. I couldn't move. Something, somewhere, was hurting.

The train, horribly distorted, had loomed ahead, ready to destroy me. I thought I was going to be minced on the tracks. In a matter of seconds . . .

Was I dreaming or was this real?

My whole body seemed immobilized, held down, but where was the train? Where was the bloody impact? Was I already dead?

I'd heard about people looking down from above, watching their dead or dying bodies below on the operating table, or in a car accident. But I felt as though I'd been dragged down, *beneath* it all.

I *must* have been dreaming . . . even though I pulled my body with all my strength, my movements were crushingly slow, just like in a nightmare.

What was happening?

8:30 pm

My eyes flew open. I was lying down flat on my back.

There was no train. There was no railway line! The train that was going to crush me beneath its screaming bulk had completely vanished, along with the train tracks and the gloomy, blue-lit tunnel! How long had I been passed out here?

I was in a small, dark space, filled with looming shapes and angles. I struggled to sit up, but my panic worsened when I felt that something tight was pinning me down. I tried to kick, but the movement hurt like crazy.

My leg! What about the gash on my leg? Surely I'd lost too much blood?

It suddenly felt like that moment up on the tracks had been hours ago . . . What had happened? I shook my head, trying to regain my senses, before looking around again. A dim, caged light on the cement ceiling above where I lay revealed several shafts running away on either side of me. Across to my right, I could see a huge metal wheel, the kind that locks and seals off gas and water pipes. Above that, there were four long pipes that ran the length of the wall and then disappeared up a dark shaft. I seemed to be in some sort of landing station in a pump room.

I was lying low, just above the floor, and my body was wrapped up tightly in an old, gray army blanket. How did I get here? I couldn't shake the cloudiness from my head to figure out what had happened, how I'd escaped the impact of the train and why I was tucked away in this dank, dark place.

My head fell back in despair. I thought I must have been caught again, and that this was some kind of dungeon. Vulkan Sligo and his lying little spy girl, Winter, had caught up with me. I'd escaped the train somehow, but I'd been recaptured and shoved in this prison.

My mind flashed back to how my foot, trapped in the heavy gumboot I'd taken from the zoo, wouldn't budge from the tracks. I was stuck there, facing an oncoming train . . . The last thing I could remember thinking was that the screeching brakes would never stop the train in time.

I realized, as the train was bearing down on

me, that I would never see my family again. I would die, never solving the mystery of the Ormond Singularity. There was a loud shriek . . . and then, just before impact, the whole world seemed to open up and I'd fallen into a gaping blackness. I felt the terrifying sensation of falling into some dark space beneath my body, as if the earth had opened up and swallowed me.

A shocking thought suddenly struck me. Maybe I *hadn't* escaped the train. Maybe both my legs were gone and I was regaining consciousness in some overcrowded prison hospital. Horrified, I finally ripped off the gray blanket that was holding me down.

I nearly passed out with relief. Both of my legs were still there!

I wiggled my toes and cringed at the pain of this simple movement. I sat up and looked closer and saw that the gash on my leg had been cleaned and covered with a semi-transparent dressing. Through it I could count seven neat stitches!

Someone had stitched the gash on my leg *and* tucked me up tightly in this blanket! Sligo wouldn't have done that for me. But who had? It didn't make sense.

The pain in my leg throbbed into my consciousness. I forced myself to breathe deeply, inhaling hard. I was alive and that had to be a good thing. But how I'd escaped being trapped on the railway tracks . . . I had no idea.

My memory was slowly becoming clearer. The ground beneath me, the metallic mesh that my foot was jammed against, had somehow given way. I'd fallen through the hole, but then someone was there and had caught me. I was in the stranger's arms, just below the tracks, as the hideous sound of the train passed right over both of us.

9:01 pm

"Who's there?" I tried to ask, suddenly aware of a shuffling sound nearby. But my voice came out as a hoarse croak. I struggled as I sat back up again to look around.

A movement against the wall across from me caught my eye. "Who's there?!" I repeated, my voice tentative, afraid of who I was about to meet.

I couldn't make out his face in the dim light, but I could see that whoever the thin figure was, he seemed to be wearing an oversized dark green suit and a tie.

The gangly figure slowly approached and I braced myself. He appeared to be very stooped, with fair, straggly hair and huge eyes, wide like a possum's.

"Did you do this?" I asked him, pointing to my stitched leg.

"I certainly did," he said, unrolling a wrapped-up piece of fabric to reveal a range of shiny medical instruments in a line. "Would you like anything else done while I have my tools out? Some minor surgery? I've got everything here. You've got no idea what people leave on trains. No idea. I've got a whole library on microsurgery back home if you'd like anything taken off or reattached?"

"No," I said hastily, cautiously drawing my injured leg away from him. "Thank you for what you've done. For helping me."

I ran my hands through my hair and exhaled, hoping like crazy that this unusual guy was on my side. "I remember," I said, "falling beneath the tracks just before the train reached me . . . and being caught."

The skinny man chuckled. "Like falling into the fiery pits?" He softly brushed some dust and dirt away that had just fallen on his array of surgical instruments before carefully rolling them back up in the cloth. "I could see you were in a bit of trouble," he said. "You were very lucky that your foot was jammed against one of the drain covers. A couple of feet further south or north and I don't think I could have helped you . . ."

"Drain covers?" I asked, thinking again of the metallic mesh on the tracks that was near my trapped foot.

He nodded vigorously, and a piece of his wispy fair hair flew up like a cockatoo's comb.

"All the underground lines have huge drains under them," he explained, "big, big tanks — otherwise the rainfall from the city above that doesn't get caught by the drainage systems would gush down and flood the lines. That's why all along the tracks you'll find drainage openings. The storm water is stored in tanks below, and when they're full they're pumped out into the city drains."

The man paused and peered up at me again, as if he were checking if I was listening to him.

"I heard you running along the line," he continued. "You stumbled, pushing that big guy off the tracks, then I saw that you'd become stuck. There wasn't much time, but I was able to yank down the drain cover from beneath you . . . and then down you came after it. I caught you, and here you are."

He grinned, looking very pleased with himself. "Right now, we're in one of the connecting tunnels that link up all the drainage tanks. They only inspect them every few months. The rest of the time they're free and open to traffic — me, that is."

"And no one saw us?" I asked anxiously. He shook his head vigorously again. This time I saw a small cloud of dust shake up in a soft shaft of light. "I owe my life to you," I said, tearing up with relief, hardly believing what had happened. "If you hadn't gotten me down here, I'd be like my shredded boot up there — all over the tracks, only in more and messier pieces."

"Now, now, don't get too carried away. I didn't want you squashed all over the tracks just up there. Didn't want fuss and bother and police and a rescue team with their great big generator lights, and ambulance people, and all that," he said. "Didn't want the bluecoats coming too close to that particular drainage tank — some of the shafts that lead off it," he said, "lead straight to my home. Didn't want that."

"Bluecoats?" I asked.

"The blue coats. The railway cops," he explained. "They wear blue like the regular cops. They were all over the place looking for you."

OK, so he's gotta know who I am, I thought to myself. Surely.

"One of those tunnels leads right to my home," he said, pointing up into the dark. "Two of them do, actually, if you count the one with the rockfall blocking it. Normally, that's the way I'd take you there."

"Sorry, take me where?" I wasn't too sure I wanted to go anywhere with this guy.

He ignored my question. "At the moment it's too dangerous to use the tunnels, just in case the bluecoats are still hanging around."

I understood that.

"It was a close call. They were crawling everywhere looking for you. They thought they were coming to scrape you off the track."

Scrape you off the track.

His words really hit me. Shock smacked home. My heart thumped against my ribs and my breath came again in big, panting sobs. I fell back, slumped now against the wall. I'd had such a narrow escape, but I was alive, thanks to this strange little guy in the suit.

"How long have I been down here?" I asked.

"You've been out of it for a while," he said. "Been asleep all day."

I felt relieved, knowing that Red Tank Top was long gone for the time being, but then I was tormented by thoughts of Winter Frey. She'd set me up, I told myself. She made up something, just to trick me and find out where I was. I wasn't sure if I'd seen a passenger in the back of the black Subaru — my focus had been on the guy jumping out of the car, coming for me — but Red Tank Top had appeared within seconds of her phone call to me, and he *almost* got me and the contents of my backpack.

My backpack! I suddenly panicked, sitting up, realizing I didn't have it.

"It's OK," my new friend said. "If you're looking for your bag, it's there, against the wall."

My eyes followed the direction of his pointed finger, and I spotted a mound near the opening of one of the shafts. I sank back with relief.

"What are those drawings all about?" he asked. "Hope you don't mind me looking at them."

"As long as they're all still there," I said. "They're really important drawings my dad did before he died."

"And what did you think you were doing," he asked, "running along the tracks like that? Looking for death, too?" His possum eyes narrowed. "You weren't looking for lost property, were you?"

"Lost property? I was running for my life. There are people chasing me."

"Yes, yes," he said, nodding. "I saw that big guy coming after you. Hardly fair. I know what that's like."

My heart rate was returning to something like normal. Winter aside, I started to feel pretty good. I'd dealt with Sligo's thug and the drawings were still safe in my backpack. I'd escaped again and was free to keep working on the dangerous mystery of the Ormonds. The DMO.

"I can't be caught by him, or anyone like him," I said. "Or by the cops, of any sort. I've gotta get away from here — if I'm caught, it's the end of everything."

"That makes two of us," said the man, chuckling. "*I* can't afford to be caught, either. That's why we're both hidden down here!"

I was a bit unnerved that this guy had only helped me to keep his secret lair safe. Still, I owed him big time. But being saved from the train wasn't going to be much use to me if the authorities were going to find me.

"What if they come down the tunnel to where we are now?" I asked.

"That's why we are about to move on," he said. "They've been searching the other drains all day and they mustn't find us here."

"Where can we go?" I asked.

"Do you think you can walk?"

"I'll give it a try," I said, carefully getting to my feet and trying some weight on my injured leg. It felt a little wobbly, but good enough.

"Good man. Grab your things and we'll be on our way."

11:07 pm

The man in the suit pushed me aside. "Me first. You follow," he ordered. "There are iron pins wedged into the stonework, all the way up the shaft. Some of them are badly rusted and loose, so pay attention to what I do — I think I remember which ones they are."

I hoped so too. I watched as he started climbing, testing each iron spike for hold before putting all his weight on it. He was a bit like a spider, slender and slight — a daddy longlegs scaling a wall.

"Where exactly are we going?" I asked again.

"Back to my place," he said. "Up this shaft." He pointed to the dark opening of the shaft in the roof of the pump station.

It was probably a good idea to lie low with this guy for a while, I thought, even though I didn't really have a clue where he was leading me. I quickly began following him up into the shaft, watching intently for the safe spikes he'd used to haul himself up, before grabbing them myself. My backpack kept getting in the way, catching on the toeholds higher up, making it just that little bit more difficult. I tried as best I could to ignore the pain in my stitched leg as I battled my way up. Even though I was helped by the light that increased the higher we climbed up the shaft, I was still falling behind and in danger of losing the mysterious man ahead.

He was almost at the top of the shaft, and I hoped he'd wait for me. I didn't know where I was going to come out — for all I knew I could have been walking straight out into the steel embrace of the police and railway officials. I kept climbing, bullying the backpack behind me, my one bare foot bruised and painful with every step I took.

11:38 pm

The light brightened, and I realized that it was the pale night sky I could see high above me.

I made it to the top of the shaft and cautiously stuck my head out and looked around. The shaft had opened up into a dusty, weed-filled yard. Another caged light about twenty yards away shone near the opening of another huge tunnel, its mouth covered by iron gates. It reminded me of the opening above the ocean I was nearly washed through in the storm floods not long ago.

My leg was aching pretty badly, but I tried to ignore it and concentrate on my surroundings and getting my bearings. Some distance away was a collection of run-down buildings against a stone cliff face, a couple of old train carriages and ancient rusting engine parts, train wheels and axles.

The guy in the suit had disappeared.

I couldn't help a brief moment of disappointment rushing through me as I realized I was alone again. He must have had second thoughts and deserted me, before I'd even learned his name.

I couldn't really blame him. He'd already done so much; it was up to me now. I should have been used to being alone. I'd have to find my way out of the old railway yards and somehow get back to a safe place.

11:40 pm

It was the middle of the night, and from where I was, the streets around the yards seemed deserted.

Still half out of the shaft, I turned to look around again for a sign of my companion.

Over at the cliff face, not far from the largest building, I was drawn to three old gray filing cabinets, each almost as tall as a man. They stood there like empty, abandoned wardrobes.

Then I heard his voice.

"Come on my boy! Over here!"

From the filing cabinet in the middle, the man in the suit beckoned to me. He was standing squashed inside it, head bowed a little to fit in, eyes in his thin face flashing with enthusiasm.

"Come on!"

This guy was a lunatic!

Now in the cold yard light I could see that his suit was very shabby. His tie looked like something out of Gabbi's dress-up box, his jacket was worn and slipping, too big, off his shoulders, while the arms crept up, too short at the wrists. If he was as crazy as he looked, he might want to slam me inside a filing cabinet too.

I crawled out of the shaft, my swollen ankle hurting, the stitches in my gashed leg pulling painfully on my skin. Dragging my backpack over my shoulder, I carefully got to my feet.

A wailing siren nearby made me drop to the ground and almost back down the shaft again. I remained crouched until the cop car had passed. Time to go. I couldn't hang around with a guy in a cabinet. I couldn't hang around at all! The cops were coming and I had to get away. My legs felt shaky and painful but my system was pumped with nervous excitement, edgy and raring to go.

Somehow, I would have to make it through the yards and onto the road without being seen. I dropped down again as yet another police car whizzed past outside the fence.

"What are you doing?" my companion called. "Come on! Get over here! You can hide here!"

Sure, I thought. Standing in a cabinet in full view — a great way to hide. He was nuts!

"Thanks again, for everything, but I've gotta go," I called. I was about to start crawling towards the cover of the old buildings when I saw something that made me doubt my own sanity.

I blinked in disbelief.

The man in the suit disappeared into the filing cabinet! And I mean disappeared into it! Swallowed up! One moment he was standing, squashed in there, the next moment — gone!

I stared, trying to work out where he'd suddenly disappeared to when another police car, siren blaring, lights flashing, whizzed by on the road, just beyond the rusty wire fence. It was fast followed by another, and another. They'd sent out the cavalry, and I knew who they were hunting.

If ever a guy needed to disappear into a filing cabinet this was the moment.

I ducked down as the wailing sirens tore through the air, and scurried like a crab towards the spot where my companion had vanished.

"Hey!" I called. "Where are you? Where did you go?"

As I spoke, he suddenly reappeared, once more framed by the cabinet. It was like a magician's trick! Before I could work it out, a nearby noise alerted me. About one hundred yards away, a group of railway police were approaching, shining their flashlights ahead of them. They were searching the buildings and it was only a matter of minutes before they'd reach us.

"Look!" commanded the thin guy. He pressed against the back of the filing cabinet and somehow it opened behind him like a door. He disappeared through the opening, and the cabinet wall snapped back into position.

I stood staring again at an empty filing cabinet!

Astonished, I watched as the back of it opened up again, and he reappeared. It was just like a secret door you'd see in movies!

"Don't just stand there! Come on through!"

I scrambled to my feet, then did exactly as he had, pushing against the back panel. I felt it give behind me. I pushed backwards, squeezing through while the false cabinet wall snapped right back into position.

I was in another world! Behind the filing cabinet was a stone cellar and I looked around in wonder, trying to work out how the guy in the suit had done this. He must have replaced the original back wall of the filing cabinet with a spring-loaded version so that it opened backwards and then snapped shut again. Then he must have placed the refitted cabinet up against a pre-existing doorway so that it hid the entrance to the cellar in which I now found myself!

Yet, from outside, it just looked like one of three discarded pieces of office furniture quietly rusting away.

He extended a thin arm from his tattered, short jacket sleeve. "Welcome," he said with a lively handshake, "to the world of The Reprobate!"

2 MARCH

305 days to go . . .

Repro's Lair

12:01 am

"The who?" I asked.

"A magistrate called me that once. 'Reprobate.' It means sinner. A bad guy." He shrugged as if he didn't mind. "The nickname stuck. You can call me Repro."

I shook his wiry hand back. "Repro," I nodded.

We were in a room about twice the size of my bedroom at home, filled with the sort of furnishings I'd become used to back in the St. Johns place. Thrown out stuff like a crooked, scratched up table and multicolored pieces of old carpet on the stone floor. And in one corner, there was an old sofa bed covered with blankets next to a long, sagging bookcase made of water-damaged wooden planks propped up on carriage parts.

Wherever I looked, small towers of boxes stacked higgledy-piggledy rose from the ground. In the gloom I could see that every surface was cluttered with strange, shadowy objects and boxes overflowing with hand tools and stuffed with documents tied with string.

A continuous, whirring sound drifted out from two old-fashioned electric fans mounted on the far wall.

I watched Repro waft with ease through the narrow spaces left between the piles of books and objects, pausing to fuss with loose papers, making tiny adjustments to the towers, running his spidery fingers softly over the many shapes as he moved.

The wooden shelves that ran along the length of the stone walls were crammed with boxes and books, folders and cans. Three long railway carriage seats ran beneath them and around a corner, providing a right-angle seating area under a light bulb that hung from some very shady electrical wiring. I traced the wiring with my eyes to see that Repro had patched it into an electricity cable running up a wall.

A string of grayish laundry and a sheet stretched across the ceiling, from the top of another filing cabinet to a hook just above the secret entrance. It formed a makeshift screen between a tiny shower recess and toilet and the rest of the cellar area.

12:05 am

Behind me, Repro pushed a huge and heavy chest against the back of the narrow pass through which we'd both just climbed.

"There," he puffed, brushing his hands together in satisfaction. "Now we're nice and cozy, and the filing cabinet's blocked off. Well, what do you think of it?" he asked, looking around with pride.

"It's cool," I said.

As I spoke, I heard a clicking, winding sound, coming from above. I looked up at the wall and watched as the tiny double doors of two cuckoo clocks flew open, and two wooden birds on their springs started sounding off. Their wooden wings clacked with every chirp.

. . . 10, 11, 12, I counted, thinking it must have been midnight. But one of the cuckoos continued, 13, 14, 15, 16, 17, until Repro reached up and smacked the small, carved bird. It retreated into its chalet, and the tiny doors slammed shut again.

"That is one crazy cuckoo," he said. "Must fix him once a day."

I looked at him in amazement. There was so

much I wanted to know about his life here in hiding. Now that I'd had a good chance to study him, it was plain to see that Repro — although skinny — was tough. His possum eyes were set in a thin, lined face that had seen a lot of life, not much of it easy, I thought.

12:10 am

A box of crackers on the wobbly table caught my attention. Even the pain in my leg couldn't distract me from how hungry I was.

I had to sit down suddenly as strength drained from my body. The after-effects of adrenaline had left me weak and shaky.

"Help yourself," offered Repro.

I grabbed the box and pulled out a couple of crackers, shoving them into my dry mouth. They were stale. I suddenly felt like throwing up.

Repro pulled a chair up to the table and sat across from me. "That gash in your leg sure was ugly," he said. "Just as well I've got a good dispensary."

"I already had an injury there," I said, not wanting to have to explain my little run-in at the zoo. "That business down on the tracks opened it up again."

Repro threw back his head and laughed.

What was funny about that? This guy was

truly bizarre. Stunned, I watched while Repro made two claws out of his sinewy hands, held them high in the air, then frightened the life out of me by roaring and pouncing at me. I jumped sideways, falling off the chair, while he continued to laugh wildly.

"I guess that means you know who I am," I said from the ground, after realizing what he was up to with his lion act.

"I wouldn't have shown you the entrance unless you were like me — on the run. How else could I trust that you wouldn't blow *my* cover? Anyway," he said, standing up again and straightening his jacket. "Let's see what we have in the way of footwear in . . . the collection."

The way he said the last two words was as if he was describing a sacred monument or a secret treasure.

"The collection?" I repeated, as I scrambled back to my feet.

"On the shelves, in the cupboards, on the floor, on the tables, on the walls, under the bed . . . that's my collection. You wouldn't believe the things I find on the trains. Somewhere in the corner there's even a skeleton, left behind by a medical student I suppose . . . imagine leaving a skeleton on the train!" He threw back his head and laughed again. "Or maybe it was a railway commuter who waited too long to get off at the right station! I have loads of excellent and valuable things over there. Including shoes — you can't go through life with one boot."

I looked down at my feet. One in an oversized gumboot, one bare, swollen and filthy.

Repro started digging through a plastic garbage bag, throwing random shoes and sneakers out behind him. "Have a look through those," he suggested. "Lost property. Left on the trains. New clothes, old clothes. New shoes, old shoes. Umbrellas, pens, pencils, art, glasses, folders, documents, phones, cards . . . you name it, it's been left on a train. And if it's been left on a train, or on a platform, I've got it here in the collection."

"And that painting?" I asked, pointing to a beautiful landscape of the harbor in much earlier times. Cute little cottages with smoking chimneys were nestled in the thick forests around the foreshore, while fluffy white clouds glowed, reflected in the peaceful blue water, rippled only by the passing of a small steamer.

"Left on the train," he said, "wrapped up in brown paper. I liked it so much I hung it on my wall. It reminds me of the world outside. Well," he added, "the good parts of the world outside."

"It's awesome," I said, understanding what he

meant about "the good parts." Until my dad died, and this life on the run began for me, I never realized just how good the "good parts" were.

"Sometimes they leave the Lost Property depot unattended," said Repro. "Duck out for a smoko — filthy habit, if you ask me. That's when I pop in to see what's in there. See if I can add anything to the collection."

He and Boges would have gotten along well, I thought, collecting all sorts of lost or abandoned bits and pieces, then giving them a new life.

From a box that had landed beside me, I found a pair of nearly-new running shoes that fit almost perfectly.

"They're yours," he said. "I'll never wear them."

"Thanks," I said excitedly. "What about these?" I picked up several wallets and lost school bus passes and waved them at him.

"Help yourself. I can't really pass as a school kid!" He giggled, flashing his big eyes. "Take whatever you like. You should take some of these, too. They make a lovely bang. You like fireworks?"

He'd passed me some metal objects that were shaped like screws, except ten times larger than the biggest screw you've ever seen, and with much bigger heads.

"Fireworks?" I asked. "Weren't they banned because they're so dangerous? Kids were blowing their hands off and stuff?"

"These are *track detonators*. Explosive caps. When the fettlers are working on the train lines, they place these along the tracks about a mile back from where they're working. When a train runs over them, they explode with a loud crack and the driver knows to slow the train down. You've heard about land mines? These are like tiny land mines. Give them a bang with a hammer and they make a great old noise!"

Repro danced around waving the detonators.

"Hey, careful," I said. "You might drop one and bring the bluecoats back here."

I took them and stashed them safely at the bottom of my backpack.

"Now don't throw that around too roughly," warned Repro, "or your backpack might go off!" He found that idea pretty hilarious, and fell forward laughing.

A sudden noise outside made him stop, mid-giggle.

From outside came the sounds of searchers approaching — people yelling out to each other just beyond the thin steel of the filing cabinet. I gripped the table. I didn't think they could hear us, but I held my breath until, slowly, the sounds faded away.

We were safe . . . for now.

11:41 am

I vaguely remembered slumping sideways, relieved and exhausted in my chair, but when I woke up I was lying across a little makeshift bed and Repro was sitting at the table with a couple of empty food containers in front of him. I felt weird — spaced out, flat.

"I thought you were dead," said Repro, casually taking his tie off and hanging it on a hook. "You've been asleep for hours. You hungry?"

I realized that the place smelled like something delicious and spicy. At the thought of food I was ravenous again.

"I've been out this morning to get some food. I've kept some for you," he said, lifting a container out of a small cooler. "It's from the Hari Krishna people — curried vegetables."

"Thanks," I said, leaping greedily off my bed and over to the table.

12:13 pm

I didn't know much about my new companion when first we met, but now he seemed determined to fill me in. By the time I'd finished eating he'd told me a great deal of his life story: how he'd been a great locksmith, a black belt martial arts master — he'd almost won the championship in Singapore some years back — and had a good business until he made a few bad decisions and went bankrupt.

"When you're down on your luck you start mixing with different people," he said. "People on the edge. And in the end, I lost everything. All I got out of it was a criminal record and some time inside. At least I eventually cleaned up my act, I try to remind myself."

His thin face saddened, but not for long. "See, I've got this gift," he said, smiling wide and showing his teeth. "I can find the right numbers to any combination lock. On the old safes, my fingers can *feel* the right numbers. It's a bit like playing an instrument. So when people used to forget their combination numbers, they'd call me. I'd keep trying different numbers until my fingers told me which numbers were used. The *used* numbers feel slightly different from the unused ones — like they want to fall into place easier. The unused numbers are stiffer. Simple really."

As Repro spoke about his gift, his fingers spread wildly over the tabletop, like they themselves were reenacting their part.

"And people used to pay me really well," he said. "And although I'm certainly not the boy I used to be when I almost won the championship in Singapore, I'm still pretty handy in a fight. Pretty handy."

"What about this place?" I asked, looking around his stone room. "And how did you know about the old shafts and the pump room in the tunnel?"

"An old guy told me about these places when I was living on the streets. There are dozens of unused and unfinished tunnels, rooms, pockets, drains and air shafts. Some of them are disused, some were never used — they were just abandoned. So when I needed to hide . . ." he looked away for a second, and when he turned back his face was clouded with remembered fear. "A few years back, a very dangerous criminal was looking for me. That's when I was forced to move in here and hide. I didn't want to be found. This crim' cuts people's toes off — he's not a gent at all."

"Toe Cutter Durham!" I shouted, shocked that Repro'd been chased by such a big-time bad guy. "I've heard all about him!"

He tapped a finger to his nose. "I recognized another fugitive in you," he said. "Like I said earlier, you're the last person who would tell the authorities about me or the collection."

I nodded, but my attention started jumping away and replaying the unbelievable things that had been happening to me. The two criminal gangs that were after me. The fact that I myself was a wanted criminal as far as the police were concerned. The fact that I had to survive for another three hundred days or so, while my little sister faded away in a hospital bed.

I felt alone and scared.

Even what was happening now seemed unreal and bizarre. Maybe I *was* losing my mind — maybe what the TV and the newspapers were saying about me was true. Was I some sort of psychopath? Maybe I *had* tried to kill Uncle Rafe and my little sister Gabbi. Maybe I was suffering from amnesia about these terrible things I'd done. I'd seen movies about that sort of thing.

I grabbed my backpack and pulled out my phone. I looked over at Repro as he raved on about his martial arts triumphs and his locksmith skills. He'd saved my life by dragging me down into the drains and into his maze of tunnels — no question. But my heart was pounding and my clothes were damp with the sweat my sudden fear had produced.

Was I really here listening to a freaky-looking guy raving on about his life story — a guy who popped in and out of a secret door in a filing cabinet? Or was this whole place some sort of hallucination happening in the mind of the psychopath that everyone thought I was?

I looked down at the Celtic ring on my finger. That was real, wasn't it? In a hospital not very far away, my little sister was lying helpless and unconscious. When she woke up, they were going to tell her I did that to her — that I tried to kill her. The thought of that nearly broke my heart. And just when I thought I had someone to trust, Winter had betrayed me. My life was a total mess. My thoughts were spinning out of control. I grabbed the sides of the table again, feeling like I might lose consciousness any minute.

12:45 pm

I turned my phone on.

📱 cal, u ok? boges.

📱 cal, pls let me know if ur ok. heard about zoo attack on radio.

📱 dude, ur killing me here! pls text me back already!

After I read Boges's messages, my phone beeped three times and then died. No battery.

Voices very close outside made us both freeze. I dropped my phone in my bag, and Repro stood perfectly still, a couple of feet away from me. There was only a thin layer of steel between us and the outside, so we could hear every word they said.

"That's odd," the first man said. "The electricity is running here. Look, you can see the disk in the electricity meter moving. It's slow, but it's moving."

"So it is. That *is* odd," the second voice agreed. "Someone around here is using power. But where? These yards and buildings have been derelict for years."

Repro hissed, "They've noticed the old meter box against the last building — it's lost its door." He swiftly dived to the floor and tugged his patched-in illegal cable out of the old electrical wiring. Even though it was bright daylight outside, we were plunged into total darkness and the whirring of the two big wall fans slowly died. I clung on to the table, scared stiff.

"Can't see anyone around here using anything," said the first voice. "No lights or machinery or anything."

"We'd better make sure," said the other. "We'd better do a thorough search. Especially with reports of that fugitive on the tracks."

In the pitch blackness I could hear my own breathing coming fast. If either of those two guys outside looked closely at the back of the filing cabinet, or pressed it, despite the heavy chest Repro had pushed against it, chances were they'd spot the secret door.

A loud noise from outside made me jump. In the darkness, I sensed Repro's anxious presence. We waited. Voices from outside came closer.

"You saw him come this way?" I heard someone ask. Whoever it was must have been right next to the filing cabinets. The sound was as clear as if the guy had been standing next to me, which in a way he sort of was.

"Just here," said the new voice. "There were two of them."

Two of them! We were goners!

"But that was last night," said the other.

"So? They're still here I reckon, hiding somewhere. No one's left the area."

"Someone's here for sure," said the first voice. "Someone's using power. Take a look at the meter box."

A pause.

"It's not moving."

"But it was a second ago! I saw it!"

"Well, it's not now. See for yourself. Might have just been a power surge or something."

"What about these old filing cabinets?"

"What about them?"

"This one here's in pretty good shape. I might

take it home with me."

Hardly breathing, I sat pressed up against the old table, trying not to move a muscle or make even the slightest sound.

I felt Repro tense with even more fear beside me as we both cringed through the sounds of the filing cabinets being tapped, pushed and banged.

Please don't let us get caught, I begged. Not only would it mean doom for me and my chances of solving Dad's mystery, but it would mean taking responsibility for ruining Repro's happy little world.

Suddenly, I heard the clicking sound on the wall above me. Oh no! Not that crazy cuckoo!

I felt Repro spring up in the darkness and give it a whack . . . but not before it squeaked out half its cuckoo sound.

"What was that?" asked one of the voices.

"Not sure," said the other. "Could've been a bird."

"In a filing cabinet?"

"Let's go," said another voice. "They're garbage. They all seem to be rusted together. Anyway, since when did you become so stingy? You can get a brand new one for fifty bucks."

Gradually the voices moved off, and we were both able to breathe again.

"That was close," said Repro, as he groped

around in the dark. In a few moments, he'd struck a match and lit two candles. "They were right outside my front door. I thought they were going to rip the whole thing out! Lucky for us that last guy spoke up, but people shouldn't be so dismissive of old stuff."

We'd had a narrow escape for sure. The candles brightened the dark interior and Repro snatched up a newspaper and held it up for me to see. "I picked this up — the latest edition — while I was out getting the food," he said. "You're one hot property, my boy. I'm afraid you can't stay here very long. I know you're in trouble, but you're too hot to stay with me."

I gulped. There was my face all over the front page, again. Sure, it was blurred and the detail was poor, but I was recognizable.

"You're a wanted criminal," Repro said. "I thought you were just involved in a little misdemeanor at the zoo. They'll be looking for you everywhere now," he said, waving the newspaper at me. "They nearly just walked right through my secret door. We can't have that, sport."

I hated hearing Repro say that, but he was right. It was a fair call. I didn't want to put him at risk again. He'd helped me too much for me to turn around and do that to him.

I studied my image in the newspaper. I'd have to work on my appearance again, which meant I'd have to rely on help from Boges.

"So much as I like the company, my boy — I love a chat — I can't afford to have you stay here. Not without some sort of reimbursement." As he said these words, he rubbed his fingers and thumb together, indicating money. "It's not just the extra food I'd have to get for you, and the drain on resources," he said, looking up at his illegal patch into the electricity cable, "but you're a hazard to be around. You seem to drag the cops with you wherever you go. I don't want any trouble. I don't want this place ever found. This is my home. Plus I'm very attached to my toes and they're very attached to me. We never want to be separated. I aim to keep all ten for the rest of my life."

Sounds outside indicated that the search party was retracing its footsteps, coming back towards the yard area and the filing cabinets. Again, we both sat still, waiting in tense silence until they passed.

Repro was making it very clear that I couldn't stay. Not while things were so hot. But this was the best hideout I'd ever seen: self-contained, secure and hidden.

I gave it one more try.

"I don't have any money, but I could be useful to you," I said. "You know, I could run messages. Be a gopher?"

"I can take care of my own arrangements, thank you, and you need to stay low, not be running around gophering. It's a pity," he said. "Would have been good if you could have stayed. It's nice having someone to chat to."

"I've got quite a story," I said, trying to tempt some more time out of him.

He grinned, cautiously. "Maybe just one more night then."

3 MARCH

304 days to go . . .

4:39 pm

I'd spent the whole day looking through the collection. Repro had gathered an amazing amount of stuff. There were golf clubs, jars of coins, buttons, beads, pins and badges, loads of books and stacks of newspapers — local *and* foreign — meticulously arranged by date and location. I found some classic novels and did some reading. Typically I would have gone straight for the thrillers, but that kind of fiction didn't seem to cut it anymore for someone with a life like mine.

I'd been engrossed in a book for a couple of hours, but my eyes kept turning to the painted landscape of the harbor on the wall. I thought it was familiar — probably a print of some very famous artist's work that we'd looked at in art class. School . . . what a distant memory.

Lazily, I looked over at Repro who was

humming to himself while toying with some sort of little motor at his table. He seemed to enjoy my company, although he was nervous all the time. My presence might have made it worse, but I was pretty sure that was just the way he was.

I was sorting through some more of Repro's books from his library on the shelf, when I noticed an old, stained, black-and-white photograph leaning against a white pillar candle in a silver dish. I picked it up to look at it and also noticed a tiny gold angel pin that was resting beside it.

"Who's this?" I called out to Repro. He looked up and squinted at the photo I was holding — a picture of a smiling woman with great big curls in her hair, leaning against an old-fashioned car.

His face fell.

"That's nothing. Put it back," he snapped.

"I'm sorry," I said, returning it to its seemingly sacred place by the candle and the pin. "I was just curious."

"No," Repro said after a moment. "*I'm* sorry. I didn't mean to bark at you . . . I'm just not used to having anyone around, looking at my stuff. See, it's a picture of my mum. We haven't spoken in a very long time."

"How come?"

"Oh . . . she wasn't happy with the way my

life was heading. This was a while ago now. She wasn't happy about the people I was mixing with . . . she was trying to change me, but I resisted. And then she stopped writing to me . . . turned her back on me after I was sent to the slammer for robbery." Repro walked over to me and picked up the picture. "Can't blame her. But I haven't seen her since," he said sadly, looking at her image.

"Have you tried to get in touch with her?"

"No. I don't want to cause her any more trouble. I've put her through enough shame."

"What's this pin?" I asked him, changing the painful subject. "Lost property?"

"Ah," he said, taking the pin and holding it up to the light. "Mum gave it to me, years ago. It's a guardian angel."

He slowly put the pin back in its place with the photo. "I don't know if the pin ever did much to protect me, but I'm still here, aren't I?" he said, with a toothy grin, "In any case, these are all I've got to remind me of her."

Repro sighed and went back to work on his motor, leaving me to wonder whether I'd end up like him . . . alone . . . away from my family, away from my mum.

11:52 pm

Before I knew it, it was late again and Repro was snoring softly on his sagging little bed. We'd played poker late into the night, after I found a deck of cards among the treasures on his shelf. He even had a shuffle machine and an almost-complete set of colored chips.

This would be the last night, I told myself. I couldn't risk it for him any longer. I'd need to move on and take myself elsewhere.

4 MARCH
303 days to go . . .

11:21 am

I packed up all of my stuff and then made myself look as good as possible with the help of Repro's bathroom and mirror. We said a quick goodbye, and I thanked Repro again for everything he'd done for me. It was obvious that neither of us was keen to return to solitude, but we both knew I needed to go.

Before I ducked through the door, he handed me a small brown paper bag. "Take this with you," he said, with a hand on my back. "Best of luck."

I hoped it wasn't the last I'd see of my new friend.

After checking that all was clear, I quickly squeezed through the secret door in the filing cabinet. On the other side I hurried away, passing the bright graffiti and the old garbage that had gathered along the ground near the stone walls. I slipped through the rusty iron gates at the yard entrance and paused for a second to look back at the gloomy space. No one would ever have guessed that such an incredible world existed there in hiding. I hoped it would stay that way for Repro.

I walked towards the city, cautiously, keeping my head down, while peering through the store windows for a glimpse of what I was looking for . . .

Stores
Liberty Square

11:56 am

I arrived at the mall and looked around for a suitable cafe . . . and there I found Florentino's.

I strolled in and took a seat at a table along the wall, right in front of a power point. Surreptitiously, while putting my bag down and picking up the menu, I plugged my phone charger in behind me and kicked my backpack in front of it.

I pulled the brown paper bag Repro gave me out of my pocket. There was something small in there, so I carefully tipped the bag upside down and watched as a tiny gold pin fell out onto the table. I picked it up and held it in my hand. It was his little guardian angel.

12:03 pm

"I'm just waiting for my friends," I said, smiling at the waitress who'd come over to take my order. She was a cute girl with spiky blonde hair and a tiny silver ring through her nose.

"No problem," she said, smiling back, before pouring me some water and moving on to another table.

12:19 pm

I drummed my fingers on the table, pretending to wait for the friends who were running late, and I occasionally glanced at the nonexistent watch under my sleeve in an attempt to look irritated. But mostly I looked around at the other people in there — some kids drinking milkshakes, two mothers with babies in strollers, enjoying a stolen coffee break . . . and then there was me — psycho kid — a wanted criminal and fugitive.

I tried to relax. I leaned over to the empty table next to me and picked up a newspaper from the untidy pile left for customers to read. A photo of Mum and Rafe instantly jumped out at me from about halfway down the page. I let my head fall into my hands. Just under this photo was another one of a little girl, her face turned away, drip stands and tubes surrounding her hospital bed, and a range of high tech monitors stacked behind her. It was Gabbi, my little sister.

". . . If you love your sister, please contact us, Cal." I read Mum's words. "We've done everything we can to help her get through this . . . but her condition hasn't changed. We need you to come home."

"Rafe Ormond, the fugitive's uncle," the paper reported, "who was also assaulted by the boy in the horrific Flood Street attacks of January, has begged his nephew to come home. In a public appearance in Richmond yesterday, he pleaded, 'Please, Cal, you know that this is not doing any good for anyone — running away like this. You need to come forward. Turn yourself in. You know that it's just a matter of time before you're caught, so please come home. We can deal with this together. You'll be taken care of, I promise. No one's going to hurt you, but every day you stay away, you're making things worse for yourself. Think of your mother. Think of your sister.'"

Slowly, I let the newspaper slip from my fingers. This new appeal from Mum and Rafe could only mean that Gabbi's condition was deteriorating.

"Are you OK?" the waitress with the spiky hair asked, looking down at me with concern. I didn't know how long I'd been sitting there just staring at the paper, head in my hands. I quickly pulled myself together.

"I've just had some bad news," I managed, pushing the newspaper out of sight.

"Your friends can't make it?"

I nodded gratefully.

"It would have been nice if they'd let you know a little bit earlier, hey?" she added. "So can I get you anything, then?"

"No thanks," I replied.

She picked up my empty water glass and turned away. I unplugged my phone, stashed the cord in my backpack and left the cafe.

1:21 pm

I found a quiet corner outside, near the bathrooms and a loading dock, and pulled my phone out. I really wanted to call home. I was longing to hear Mum's voice, just to tell her I was still OK . . . but I wasn't even sure what *home* was anymore. I considered calling Rafe's place but I hesitated, worried more than ever about being tracked by the police.

Instead, I called Boges, grateful again for him and his untraceable phone.

"Boges, it's me!" I said, when he answered.

"Hey man, where have you been? I've been trying to contact you for days! It's not good to leave me nothing but my imagination—I thought maybe you'd been captured by one of the gangs and murdered or something. Then I overheard someone at school saying something about you being attacked by a lion at the zoo! It was all over the news and the radio. Dude, what are you doing?!"

"My phone's been dead. Boges, listen. I'm really worried about Gabbi. I just saw an article in the paper and a picture of her where she's surrounded by all this . . . medical junk."

"Things aren't going so great with Gabs, Cal. Your mum said the doctors have been trying different ways to stimulate her recovery, but nothing's working. There's been no reaction. Your mum also said something about finding you so that you can talk to her."

"What? That doesn't make any sense. I'm the one who's supposed to have tried to *harm* her and they want me to *talk* to her?!"

"I know your mum's said some crazy stuff about you, Cal, but I don't know if she really believes that you harmed her . . . or maybe just not intentionally . . . I don't know, she's very up and down."

I wasn't convinced. Nothing at all had suggested to me that Mum believed any part of *my* story.

"They just want me to come in so they can grab me and lock me away," I said. "I reckon the police are using Mum and Rafe, and even Gabbi, to get at me. They're probably trying to make it look like I can just stroll on home, apologize, hug the family, then hold out my hands while they carefully place the handcuffs on my wrists and then help me into the paddy wagon. The reality is that they'll do whatever they can to get me behind bars, and they sure aren't going to be gentle about it."

Neither of us said anything for a long moment. I sat down on an upturned milk crate near a dumpster.

"Boges," I continued finally, "I hate to ask you again, but I really need some money. You don't know what it's like trying to survive on the streets without it. Other people can get some sort of social security payment. But I can't."

"Dude, I know. I'll do what I can. But I've gotta tell you, I'm being watched like a prime-time movie, and the cops have been here again, questioning me and my mum."

"What did they want?"

"The same old stuff. They keep asking me

questions like when did I last see you, have I heard from you at all, where do I think you could be hiding — that sort of thing. They also asked me if I wanted to help you, being your best friend and all. I've had no choice but to act cool, and pretend like I don't want to help out a criminal. It's hard. I'm trying to be convincing, but they're very suspicious of me."

He paused before speaking again. "There's definitely someone watching our place. Lately there's always this dude in a silver sedan parked in the street. He just sits there, pretending to do stuff — read a newspaper, talk on his phone, and write up reports."

Boges was so good. The best guy I could imagine to have on my side through this. But if they were watching him, I'd have to be even more careful. So would he.

"You know what to do," I said, "must be a pro by now. Just keep on changing your tracks, and never let your guard down."

"Yeah, you too."

"Can you also see if you've got some antiseptic and bandages lying around?"

"It's true?!" Boges shouted down the line in disbelief. "You were attacked by a lion? Unbelievable . . ."

I had to laugh. It was pretty crazy.

"I'm OK, now," I said, thinking back to my recovery in Repro's lair. "Luckily I stumbled across someone like me who was able to help me out. Just wait until you hear about the train incident."

"Why? Don't tell me you hijacked a train?"

"A train almost hijacked me!" I said, before briefly describing the chase with Red Tank Top.

"I'm just at the front window now," Boges said, "and that silver sedan is there again. The driver is the same guy who was watching us at Memorial Park."

I remembered the big boofhead and how I'd helped Boges get past him. I didn't like the sound of him being on the job outside Boges's place.

"You've got to keep them off your back, Boges." And mine too, I thought. How long was it going to be like this? For the rest of the year? Like the crazy guy warned me?

"Yep. I gotta go, but as soon as I can get out under the radar," said Boges, "we can try and meet up. Where are you staying?"

"I don't know." I ran my hands through my hair in frustration, and turned away from a guy wheeling a box up to the back of a truck nearby. "I've gotta get out of this town, I'll be safer if I do that. I think I've gotta start making my way to Great-uncle Bartholomew's place in Mount

Helicon. I don't know what else to do. I'm going to try the St. Johns place for now. Maybe see you soon?"

"Absolutely."

4:39 pm

I walked around, restless, unhappy and wondering when and how I was going to get out of the city. I knew that Sligo's people could be watching the bus depot again, and rail travel was too expensive. Ages ago, Mum had made me promise I would never hitchhike, but sometimes rules have to be broken — especially when you're living on the street.

Eventually I made my way back to the St. Johns Street house, keeping to the back alleys behind the city. Along the way, I followed old factory walls that were covered in layers of graffiti.

It wasn't long before I saw it again.

For some reason, this tag really bothered me. I felt a strange connection to it. Maybe I should adopt it as my motto, I thought.

Hideout
38 St. Johns Street

6:12 pm

Before closing in on the house, I circled it, checking out every street, approaching it and then doubling back, making sure no one was following me, and making sure the old house itself was empty.

Inside the front yard, I crept past the windows, listening carefully while hiding in the dense, wild overgrowth. It sounded clear so I dropped to all fours and crawled through the bushes and under the rotting porch.

From under the floorboards, I listened carefully again. I couldn't hear a thing, so I breathed a big sigh of relief, pushed away the carpet and pulled myself up through the floorboards.

The place was empty, but someone, or a bunch of someones, had definitely been in there again. A fire had been made on an old piece of metal in the middle of the room, and one of my chairs had been used for firewood. Its charred remains made the room stink of old smoke. Part of the walls and ceiling were black.

7:25 pm

When it was nearly dark, I dragged some of the garbage out the back door, down through the jungle of the backyard. A dark purple flower, one of a number on a vine that had spread over part of the fence, caught my attention. For some reason it reminded me of Winter Frey and her floaty skirt with the tiny bells, and how she'd just dissolved into moonlight that night at the Memorial. I stood there for a few moments, then went back inside.

Finally, with a little more room to move, I spread out my sleeping bag, and tried to put the troublesome girl out of my mind.

5 MARCH
302 days to go . . .

8:03 am

The staccato sounds of helicopters shuddered across the sky and I wondered if they were looking for me. How long would this place be safe? Somehow, I couldn't see myself staying here until December 31, when this curse would hopefully end.

I couldn't get back to sleep, so I got up to have a good look at my leg, which was healing pretty well. I cleaned it as best I could and re-bandaged it, tearing up another old T-shirt.

As I tried to wash some of my clothes in the sink, rubbing hard at the stained and torn fabric, the ring that Gabbi had given me knocked on the cracked porcelain, reminding me again of everything and everyone I was missing.

I pulled out the drawings for the first time in a few days and I stared at them, running a finger over my dad's work. I started thinking about the empty jewelry box inside Dad's suitcase from Ireland that we found after the break-in back home. My enemies had questioned me about a jewel that might have come from a jewelry box, but they had not mentioned anything about the cenotaph, or the Piers Ormond stained glass angel — although they were very interested in knowing more about an angel. What jewelry had that empty box contained? Was that what everybody was chasing me for?

And what was the meaning of Kilfane and G'managh — the two names on the tracing paper I'd also found in Dad's suitcase? I wished I could have gone to another internet cafe to look them up, but I couldn't risk it after seeing all the wanted stickers with my face on them, plastered around the place the last time I jumped online. I'd have to call Boges again. Get him to look them up, and let me know how my blog was going.

Frustrated and as baffled as ever, I swept the drawings out of my sight and tried to go back to sleep.

9:13 pm

I sat up, panting in the dark, not knowing how long I'd slept until I checked my phone. The old nightmare had been floating around again, but this time the threadbare, white toy dog had been joined by a giant shark. In the dream, the ground suddenly fell beneath me, like the train tracks had when Repro saved me, but this ground turned into a raging ocean. I was struggling to tread water when I realized that there was someone drifting away in the distance who looked exactly like me.

8 MARCH

299 days to go . . .

8:12 am

I could hear Boges crawling under the house so I pulled the carpet back from the floorboards. Seconds later his round face emerged, and he crawled out of the hole, straightened up and brushed himself down.

"Man," he said, looking up at the charred, blackened ceiling, "what happened here? Too lazy to take the campfire outside, huh? Or turning to pyromania now? Another one for your rap sheet?"

"There have been a few people through here, I think. I just hope they don't come back too soon," I said, relieved to see my friend, the one visitor I could trust.

Boges plopped himself down on the floor and against the wall, arms folded behind his head. "Your mum's completely moved into your uncle's place," he said.

"Actually," I reminded him, "it's her place now."

"Right," said Boges. "That is a really cool thing your uncle has done for your family. Signing over his house, sorry, his *mansion*," he corrected himself, "is a pretty huge deal." He shook his head and whistled, probably thinking back to the day we rode our bikes to Rafe's huge place in Dolphin Point, so that I could sneak in and find the drawings . . . Actually, Boges was probably thinking back to the hot yellow Ferrari we'd spotted parked outside on the street.

"Here's the antiseptic," said Boges, passing me a small tube. "And I found these, as well," he added, showing me a couple of rolls of thin bandages. They looked pretty old, but they were still sealed in plastic.

"Perfect," I said.

"I feel like moving in with you," said Boges. "You don't know what it's like at school these days. Miss Pettigrew's been on my back. Always trying to get me to make appointments with her."

"Miss Pettigrew?" I asked, trying to picture a teacher with that name. "Oh, the school counselor?" I said, remembering a brief chat I'd had with her one day shortly after Dad had passed away. "Why?"

"She thinks — *they all think* — I need counseling."

"Because of *me*?"

"Miss Pettigrew thinks I'm scarred for life, having my best friend turn into a homicidal maniac."

"Gee, thanks."

"Any time, dude. And then all the heavies are trying to be friends with me. Sean Halloran and Jake Arena —"

"Arena? Wasn't he arrested last summer?"

Boges nodded, with an almost-pleased-with-himself grin.

"And Maryanne has been showing off this ring that she said you gave her just before you went crazy and on the run."

"I've never given Maryanne Helfgott anything except distance!" I said. "*She* must be crazy."

"The principal is really riled up about the graffiti in the boys' bathroom. Someone's written 'Cal Rox' all over the brickwork above the sinks." Boges leaned up and slapped me on the back. "Dude, you may be gone, but you sure aren't forgotten!"

"Hey, I'm not completely gone . . . yet!" I said, slapping him back. "I can't get over Maryanne," I said. "Making up something like that."

"She's only trying to impress Madeleine Baker. Not that it's working. Maddy doesn't even know who Maryanne is!" he laughed.

"But Maddy knows who Bodhan Michalko is, doesn't she?!" I teased my friend. I rarely used Boges's real name — he didn't like it too much. At the same time he didn't seem too fazed about the Maddy comment. He was actually grinning.

"She's not that bad, you know," Boges defended his new friend. "Maddy's not just hot, she's smart. Anyway," said Boges, changing the subject, "you have no idea what I had to do to get here . . . Next thing, I'll be jumping over the rooftops *Mission Impossible*-style. That dude is still parked across the street in his silver sedan and still reading his newspaper — he's got no idea that this little black duck has flown the coop. I don't know whether he's with the cops, Oriana de la Force or Vulkan Sligo. You are *sooooo* stinking popular."

It was a popularity I sure could have done without.

"Let me have a look at your leg," said Boges, emptying some food out of his bag for me.

I carefully pulled up the leg of my pants.

Boges whistled. "That's gross, dude."

"You should have seen it last week."

Boges raised his round, dark eyes to me. "Respect, dude," he announced. "That is awesome. But I have one question for you: *Why*," he said, slowly and disbelieving, "did you climb into a lion's den? Bad idea. Don't you think you've already got enough trouble without baiting the king of the jungle?"

"You think I knew it was a lion's den?! It just looked like a bit of vacant land when I climbed over. Like it was awaiting development. As if I would have climbed in if I had known there was a lion waiting in there for me! I didn't have enough money for a ticket, and all I was thinking about was making my meeting with Dad's nurse, Jennifer Smith. I've got to do whatever it takes to get information!"

I suddenly felt a surge of fury. "I'm going crazy here, not knowing what to do each day. I'll do anything that's going to take me closer to getting me and my family out of this mess. *You* tell me, Boges — you're the smart one — why is all this happening? To me and my family? What am I supposed to do?"

Boges looked down and fiddled with the laces on his sneakers, shocked at my explosion.

"I'm sorry," he said. "I really am. I wish I could find a way to fix all this up for you. It's not easy."

I felt really bad then that I'd taken my anger out on him. It wasn't his fault. Without him, I'd have been captured ages ago. Or dead.

"I just wish I could see Gabbi," I said, my anger subsiding. "That's the hardest part. Will you please go and visit her, Boges? Talk to her? She might respond to your voice. She always thought you were the best."

"Sure," said Boges. "I'll ask your mum if I can go with her. She practically lives at the hospital."

Boges frowned in the direction of my backpack where it had fallen sideways, spilling out some of the stuff from inside. "What's that?" he asked.

One of the packets of tranquilizing syringes had fallen out, and I passed it to him.

"Tranquilizers," I said. "I grabbed a handful of them from a lab at the zoo. It's what saved me in my fight with Red Tank Top — the thug chasing me on the tracks. Repro gave me some railway detonators, too."

"Repro?"

"The guy who pulled me from the train tracks," I said, realizing we hadn't talked about him and his underground hideout.

"Repro — sounds like some sort of superhero name," said Boges. "Was he wearing a cape, and undies over his tights?"

I laughed, and pictured Repro in his ratty-looking suit. "Far from it. Repro is short for 'reprobate,'" I said, knowing that I wouldn't have to give Boges a dictionary definition of the word.

"Cool. So he gave you explosives?"

"Yeah, he has this huge stash of stuff he's collected from the trains and the yards. I thought I could save them for a rainy day. They could be useful."

"What about the drawings?" asked Boges. "You still poring over them?"

"Yeah, I'm starting to hate the sight of them." I grabbed my backpack and peeled back the adhesive that sealed the cut I'd made in the lining. "I keep them in here, now."

Carefully, I lifted the folder out.

Boges stared at the drawings again and pulled out his black notebook. "Whatever these mean," he said, "we both know it's huge — whatever the secret is that your dad found out about." Boges glanced down at his notes, studying the written list he'd made. "How about we go over everything we have so far on the DMO one more time."

"OK, so we've got the angels," I said, laying the two angel drawings next to each other on the floor to the left.

"And so far, we know about Piers Ormond — who we still need to look up — and the cenotaph Memorial. He may also be wearing a medal of some sort, which," he leaned in and pulled out another sketch, "brings us to this — a collection of things that can be worn."

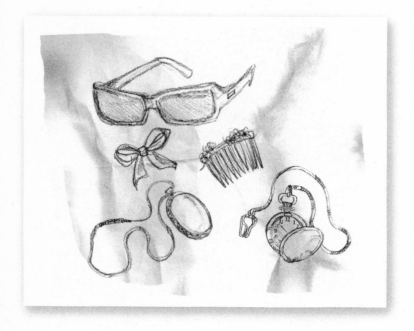

"That's right, possibly hinting at the jewel or whatever was taken from Dad's suitcase in the robbery," I said, pulling out the next one and laying it on the floor.

"The cards on the waiter's tray add up to a blackjack, a 21, which could mean something related to the word 'blackjack,' or maybe the number 21. Plus we think Dad was trying to hint at a riddle because of this," I said, adding the fifth drawing to the lineup.

"And don't forget the Roman dude," Boges reminded me. "We don't know too much about him just yet — except that it could have something to do with importance, or history, or someone in power — but we do know that people are demanding answers about the Ormond Riddle. So far, on the Ormond Riddle, we know that it's hard to track down. It sounds like it was some sort of rhyme or poem, but I still haven't been able to find anything on the words. Your dad could also have even been trying to say something about the numbers 4, 2 and 3, from the Sphinx riddle —"

"Yes, what goes on 4 legs, then 2 legs, then 3 legs?"

"Exactly, a human being. Or he could have been suggesting Oriana de la Force — remember what I told you about the psycho female Sphinx? Half-woman, half-lion?"

I nodded, and spread out the last three sketches. "And what about these?"

"We've got the '5' in the oval above the door, too," said Boges.

"Yes, and let's not forget this," I said pulling the tracing paper out of the bottom of the sleeve in my bag.

"Can you look these names up for me?"

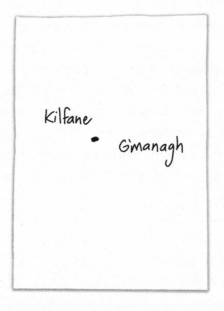

A noise from somewhere alerted me. I frowned. "Did you hear that?" I hissed.

I went to the crack near the door and squinted through it, checking outside. Everything seemed quiet.

"There's nothing out here. Are you sure you weren't followed?"

"As sure as I can be. I changed my look twice on the way here," he said, pulling out a pair of dark sunglasses and the grungiest-looking hat you've ever seen — the sort of hat that really old guys wear when they go fishing, made out of canvas or something.

I picked up the glasses and put the hat on and went to the cracked mirror in the old bathroom. Every time my reflection looked back at me, I gave myself a shock.

"Can I keep these?" I asked.

"Be my guest," said Boges. "Cal? You're looking a little intense over there. You OK?"

I looked away from my reflection and over to Boges. His round face crinkled into a frown that I knew too well, where the two lines above his nose met and deepened into one.

"I can't stop thinking about the kid I saw at the basketball courts that day," I said.

Boges let out a big sigh.

"I'm serious, Boges. He was my double. I

know it doesn't make sense, but that doesn't mean it didn't happen."

"Dude, you've been under a lot of stress. Maybe it *was* some sort of hallucination. It can happen, you know. You've been through a lot in the last couple of months. No one could blame you for making a mistake."

"I know what I saw, and I saw *me*. My face staring back at me." Boges looked unconvinced. "He was real! I've heard that everybody has a double —"

"Yeah, I've heard a lot of stupid stuff, too. It's not true," said Boges. "It's just one of those urban myths they make up. Like crocodiles in the sewers."

"I know what I saw. A kid that was identical to me. Like my twin."

"Dude, get a grip. You don't have a twin."

"And I've always had this dream," I began, knowing that if Boges already thought I was nuts, I'd have nothing to lose by telling him this, ". . . actually it's not a dream, it's a nightmare, and it's been around for as long as I can remember. There's this white toy dog and a baby screaming . . . and, for some reason, they've always scared me more than anything else."

I gripped the sides of the sink with my hands and looked again at my reflection. "The dreams seem to be getting worse," I continued. "The other night I had it again only this time I was running through this house of mazes, like some messed-up funhouse, trying to find the crying baby. And then when I finally found him, crouched, sobbing in a corner, hugging the white toy dog, he turned to look up at me . . . and he had *my* face!"

Boges frowned. "Listen. No matter what happens, what you think you see, what you dream, *this*," he banged on the drawings spread in front of him, "is the main game."

"I know you think it's weird!" I shouted, frustrated that he was being so dismissive.

"It's true, I do think it's weird! I don't know what it means. I can't explain it, but I just think that getting to the bottom of *this*," he banged on the drawings again, "will get you out of this mess you're in. Discovering the truth about the Ormond Singularity, the Riddle and the Angel. That's what you need to focus on if you want to clear your name and get your family, and your life, back."

"That's if we ever *do* get to the bottom of it," I said. "That's if Vulkan Sligo and Oriana de la Force don't get there first."

Boges whacked me on the back like he does when he's trying to cheer me up.

"Dude, you've stayed safe so far. You've got me on your side. Your dad was *relying* on you to solve this." He lowered his voice, very serious again. "Maybe the crazy guy on the street on New Year's Eve had a *real* message for you."

"I've been taking him quite seriously!" I said, with a half laugh. "His warning has probably turned out to be the most honest thing any stranger has said to me lately. I just wish the 365 days were over already!"

I slid down against the wall, landing in an uncomfortable squat. *Who was that guy anyway? And how would he have known anything about Dad?*

"I've been doing a lot of research on the Net," said Boges, interrupting my thoughts, "and I found a lot of references to the Ormond Riddle. But that's all they are. Just references. Like I said before, I can't find the *words* of the Riddle. Not anywhere. And one of the websites suggested that the words of the Riddle have been lost. So I don't know what we're going to do."

"The words of the Riddle — they've got to be somewhere," I said, "even if they're not on the Net. Rafe had written a note about it. He must know something."

"I don't think that proves anything. Just

that he knows the name of it."

Boges pointed to the drawing of the Sphinx again.

"You've got to get to your great-uncle to see if he knows something."

"Yeah, Great-uncle Bartholomew," I said. "I've gotta get out of the city. Get to his place at Mount Helicon. I've been meaning to do that ever since I snuck back to the house to get his address that night. If anyone knows anything about our family secrets it'll be him. He might know the words of the Riddle or at least know where we can find them. And he might be able to tell me more about the great-aunt that Dad mentioned once or twice."

Boges scratched his head and nodded. "So what's your uncle like?"

"I'm not really sure," I said, trying to think back to the last time I saw him. "When I was little, we all drove out to visit him at his place in the country, but I hardly recall anything about it. I think the only reason I remember him at all is because Dad was always talking about the awesome plane he was building."

"He was building an airplane?" Boges asked, clearly impressed. "Awesome!"

"Yeah, he spent all his money and his time on it, Dad also used to say."

"Well, he must have finished it by now, right? If you're lucky, he might even take you on a joy ride!"

"I'll be happy as long as I make it to his place alive, and he doesn't want to call the cops when he realizes who his visitor is."

"There's only one way to find out how he'll react. You've really gotta get out of town, dude."

That should be easy, I thought, with every cop in the state looking for me.

11 MARCH

296 days to go . . .

Liberty Square

2:04 pm

Boges was carrying his laptop bag and wearing aviator sunglasses and a cool-looking gray fedora when we met again. Beside him I felt like a complete dweeb wearing the old canvas hat and big glasses.

It didn't really bother me though, it was just so good to be walking alongside my friend again in public. Nobody seemed to be paying any attention to us, but that didn't mean I was about to let my guard down.

We turned the corner, heading for the large library building, with its white columns and cool, shaded areas.

"Some weird chick's been hanging around my place," said Boges, as we made our way up the stairs. "I've noticed her a couple of times now, just wandering outside on the street. She's definitely not a local."

Alarm bells started going off in my brain. "What does she look like?" I asked.

"Sort of cool. Sort of goth, but not exactly. Sort of, drifty . . . Hard to say."

"Eyes?" I asked.

"Two of them," said Boges, glancing at me. "She also seemed to have thin, silver ribbons through her dark hair, and tiny bells on her skirt."

"That would be Winter," I said.

Boges gave me a hard look. "Why would Winter be hanging around my place?" he asked. "Is she spying on me?"

I tried to brush his question aside.

"Maybe you should ask her next time," I said.

Liberty Square Library

2:28 pm

Boges started deleting the junk messages that were clogging my blog. A lot of people had contacted me since I last checked, but there was nothing too exciting in there, nothing that was going to really help me out of my situation.

A couple of the messages drew my attention more than the others:

Hello, Callum

Contact Cal
Messages for Cal

| Write on Callum's Wall | Messages for Cal |

J@s &T@sh:
we saw u on the news, stuck in the
lion's cage! ☹ hope ur ok now!
keep smiling ☺
xx Jasmine and Natasha xx

Hello, Callum

Contact Cal
Messages for Cal

| Write on Callum's Wall | Messages for Cal |

maryanne_rox_ur_sox:
everyone here at school thinks ur
crazy, but not me . . .
miss u . . . m

My spirits lifted a little as I read the words of support. Even the message from Maryanne Helfgott made me feel better.

Boges rolled his eyes when he read her message. "You've got quite a following. You should record an album. Seriously, you're a star. I could do backup vocals for you. Cash in on some of your fame? What do you think, huh?"

"I don't think so, buddy."

Next we started searching for the Ormond Riddle — just in case something new had come online.

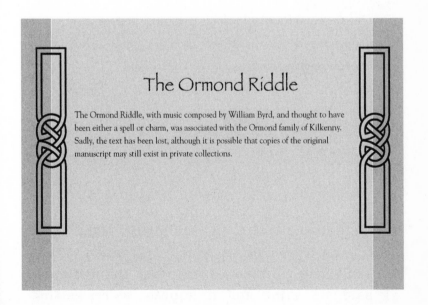

The Ormond Riddle

The Ormond Riddle, with music composed by William Byrd, and thought to have been either a spell or charm, was associated with the Ormond family of Kilkenny. Sadly, the text has been lost, although it is possible that copies of the original manuscript may still exist in private collections.

"Kilkenny," that's the name of Great-uncle Bartholomew's property in Mount Helicon," I said.

"He must have named it after Kilkenny in Ireland. Here's something," said Boges, and I leaned closer to read what he had up on the screen.

The Ormond Riddle—a riddle consisting of eight lines—appeared in the sixteenth century, and is thought to have originated in Tudor England.

"Big deal," I said. "A riddle with eight lines. Could be *Three Blind Mice*," I groaned. "That doesn't help us. Like all the other connections," I said, "I think for a minute we're getting somewhere and then I realize we're back where we started — still in the dark and still totally confused."

"Come on," said Boges, thumping me on the back, "cheer up. We're going to work this out. We have to."

We spent a little more time searching for something about the Ormond Singularity but we couldn't find anything. The problem with search engines is that you have to know what you're looking for — know what questions to ask. And we didn't know. All we had were the notes we'd made about the drawings and the drawings themselves. All we had were bits of paper.

"Try 'Piers Ormond,'" Boges suggested. "We should check up on him. He might have been some sort of hero, to get a memorial like that."

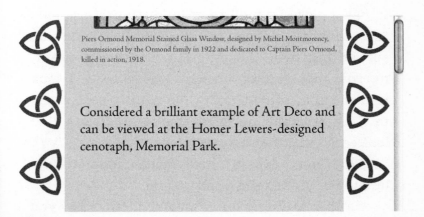

Piers Ormond Memorial Stained Glass Window, designed by Michel Montmorency, commissioned by the Ormond family in 1922 and dedicated to Captain Piers Ormond, killed in action, 1918.

Considered a brilliant example of Art Deco and can be viewed at the Homer Lewers-designed cenotaph, Memorial Park.

I looked at Boges and he looked at me. "We sorta knew that already," I said.

"But we should make a note of it."

More paper piling up, I thought. Like Oriana de la Force's desk. She'd had piles of paper and files. But she was a lawyer and that was hardly unusual. We needed *action*.

Boges looked at his cell phone, checking the time. "I've gotta start heading home. Besides, you should go, too — school will be out soon and this place will start to get busy. I'll check up the tracing paper names later, OK?"

He was about to put his phone away, when he started scrolling through his photographs. "I nearly forgot. I took this for you. Your mum let me go with her the other night."

He turned the screen of the phone to face me. It was a close-up picture of my little sister's pale face, looking as if she were asleep. Her hair was spread out over the pillow, and a transparent, narrow tube snaked up her nose. Slowly, I took it from him, staring at it for a long moment. I felt my stomach lurch at the sight of her. She looked so small and so helpless.

"You can have it," said Boges, immediately bluetooth-ing it to my cell phone.

"Is this the only one?" I asked. "Or have you got more?"

"Just that one," he said.

After saving Gabbi's picture on my phone I accidentally clicked on the thumbnail of the photo I'd taken of Oriana de la Force when I'd been up the tree outside her window. It opened up to fill my screen and I was about to close it down, when I noticed something in the photo I hadn't seen before.

I frowned. "Look," I said, pointing to the small screen, and turning it so Boges could see. "There's something written there."

The phone had focused much better on some papers on Oriana's desk, rather than on the redheaded woman herself, and I could just make out what looked like a piece of creamy paper on her desk with pale gray lettering across it. I peered closer to see what it was, then passed it to Boges.

"There's definitely something written there," said Boges. "But it's too blurry. Here," he said, opening up his laptop, "let's see what I can do. Let me play with it a bit."

Boges quickly connected my phone to his laptop with a camera download cable. I watched as he opened the picture in one of his programs.

"I've got a pretty hot photo lab program," he said, working fast, fingers flying, editing and enhancing the photograph. I sat leaning over him, watching him work.

He concentrated on the area of creamy paper on the desktop, zooming in and sharpening the contrast, so that the blurry gray letters on the top page of the pile of papers on Oriana's desk slowly strengthened, defined and took shape.

"Well, what have we got here?" he said, and I could hear the excitement in his voice. "Take a good look, my man."

I did. And what I saw gave me a thrill. The page wasn't quite in the frame, and some of the letters had been cut off, but what Boges had brought up were five unmistakable letters: I-D-D-L-E.

We looked at each other.

"What if she's got it?" I asked, my heart pounding with excitement. "What if Oriana de la Force has got the text — the *actual words* of the Ormond Riddle? She might have one of the rare copies. Someone in her position might have collected it!?"

"That's what I'm wondering too, dude," said Boges, his eyes shining. "Whoa! I'm outta here!" he said, suddenly remembering the time. "Mum'll go ballistic!"

"We've gotta get into Oriana de la Force's place," I said, as he packed up his gear. "I want to get into her study — find that piece of paper."

"And how do you think you're going to do that?" asked Boges, raising his eyebrows at me as if to say, *here comes trouble*. He slung his laptop into its case and over his shoulder.

"I've got a plan," I said, "but . . . I'm going to need some money."

I hated begging like this, especially having to scrounge off my friend. But until I could manage to get some sort of income, I was forced to do it.

"Here," said Boges, pulling thirty dollars out of his pocket. "I managed to score this for you."

"Thanks," I said, taking it, "but I'm thinking I need a lot more than that for what I want to do."

"Maybe we can both get some contract work from my uncle. Without him knowing about you, of course. He reckons I'm good enough to go out on my own. We could borrow his cleaning gear and I could tell him I'm getting a mate from school to help out with the job."

"I'll do anything, anytime," I said, pocketing the money.

I scanned the faces in the library, all of a sudden aware of someone looking our way. Sure enough, one of the librarians was staring intently at me and whispering to her colleague beside her.

"Boges," I said quietly and calmly. "I think I've been spotted. Let's get outta here."

As discreetly as I could, I indicated the two librarians. Boges looked across at them. "You're right. Looks like they're discussing you. Time we were gone," he said.

Luck was with me for once. One of the librarians was interrupted by a phone call, and the other by a mother and child with a mountain of picture books. Grateful for the distractions, we dashed over to the front door and out.

3:15 pm

We hurried away from the library and Boges took off in one direction, and I in another. Before we separated, he reminded me to try calling Eric Blair — Dad's old work colleague — again. I pulled my sunglasses on and my hat down low, and cautiously made my way through the heat and noise on the street, hoping that nobody was paying any attention to me.

3:38 pm

"Hello, Eric Blair, please," I said into the receiver. I'd stopped at a pay phone near a street corner, to try my luck again with a guy who'd hopefully have some information on Dad's trip to Ireland.

"I'm afraid Eric's still off on sick leave," the receptionist advised. "Would you like me to put you through to Wayne Slattery instead?"

Eric was still on sick leave? What was wrong with him?

"When will Mr. Blair be returning to the office?" I asked.

"Hopefully soon," she replied, dismissively. "Wayne is managing Eric's work at the moment, so I'm sure he could handle your query, if you'd like me to put you through?"

"No, thank you," I said, before hanging up the receiver with a clang — Wayne would definitely not be able to help me with *my* query.

I really didn't want this guy to turn out to be a dead end. I needed to talk to him . . . see if he had any information for me . . . but what had happened to him? What was wrong with Eric?

4:00 pm

I dreaded returning to St. Johns Street, but then I thought of Oriana and the words on the piece of paper on her desk . . . It was possible that the words to the Ormond Riddle were in her study, just waiting for me to collect them.

I hoped my plan would work.

14 MARCH

293 days to go . . .

Hideout
38 St. Johns Street

8:00 pm

The new break with the Ormond Riddle — well, *I-D-D-L-E* — appearing on a piece of paper on Oriana's desk had distracted me from my trip to Mount Helicon, yet again. It was going to be a few days before Boges would be free again, but I definitely thought this potential piece of information was worth sticking around for.

By flashlight and with the aid of the cracked mirror, I applied some cheap, temporary black dye to my short hair. I'd bought it earlier from a little city supermarket. My hair looked like one big oil splat on top of my head, reminding me of the day I first met Sligo . . . and Winter . . . the day I narrowly escaped death in an oil tank.

Winter.

If she was only going to deceive me now, why had she helped me in the first place?

I leaned my head over the sink and rinsed the blue-black dye out of my hair. I watched the dark color trails weave their way down the sink, slowly becoming paler, until eventually the water ran clear.

I smoothed my hair straight down so I looked like a real dork. When I put on a pair of round, black-rim glasses from Repro's collection, I looked like Harry Potter on a bad day. But that didn't matter. Just as long as I didn't look like me.

What would Winter think of me if she could see me now, I wondered. She'd probably laugh, I decided. Boges definitely would. Maybe I'd been a bit heavy-handed with the dye. I always thought it would be best to go for subtle changes in appearance with the use of props, rather than clumsy attempts at disguise. At least this one would wash out soon enough.

10:25 pm

I lay back on my sleeping bag, still going over my plan to get into Oriana's place. I couldn't wait to speak to Boges, and I couldn't wait to get inside the house . . . once more.

17 MARCH

290 days to go . . .

9:12 am

The ringing of my phone made me jump. I grabbed it and saw that it was a call from a private number.

I picked it up, and waited to hear who it was.

"Cal?"

"Jennifer?" I asked, tentatively.

"Yes, it's me, Cal."

"I've been hoping so bad that you'd call again!" I rushed the words out so fast that it must have sounded like one indecipherable moan — I couldn't help myself, I'd been waiting, hoping, to speak to her again ever since I missed the meeting with her at the sundial.

"I *was* there at the zoo," I began explaining. "I tried so hard to make it, and I really was almost there but . . . then I ran into some trouble."

"It's OK," she said. "I know all about that now. Forget it. Let's just hope that the third time is lucky. Cal, can we meet up tomorrow night, after I've finished work? There'll be no one around to give you trouble. Just you and me."

I didn't quite like the sound of that. It was one thing to meet someone in broad daylight, in a public place, but it was quite another thing to meet someone all alone at night in a strange place. I'd learned that lesson from our first failed meeting, when Oriana and her thugs grabbed me.

"I'm guessing you're not talking about the zoo then. Where do you work now?" I asked, cautiously. "At another hospital?"

"No, I haven't nursed for some time now. I've been working in laboratories. Right now I work at the government labs just outside of town. Do you know the Labtech Complex? Big white building? There's a bus that leaves from Liberty Square. You get off at Long Reef, and it's only a short walk down from there."

"I can figure it out," I said.

"I'm happy to work late and wait around for you. How about you come around 8:30–9 pm? You'll have to hang around until everyone's gone, but the parking lot should be empty by then. And then it'll be safe for you."

I was liking this less and less. I didn't like that this meeting was on her terms, and on her turf, again. But did I have a choice? Was it really going to be *safe for me*?

"You'll need to press the after-hours buzzer," Jennifer added, "and I'll let you in. You'll find the red button just to the right of the front entrance doors."

I thought about it for a moment.

"Cal? Are you there?" she asked.

"OK. I'll see you then," I said, and hung up, hoping I wasn't going to walk right into a trap.

18 MARCH

289 days to go . . .

Bus stop
Liberty Square

7:11 pm

The bus shelter was littered with bits of green ribbon from yesterday's St. Patrick's Day festivities. I cleared a space to sit down and turned my back on the poster of my face that had been freshly stuck up on the wall. I didn't think it looked anything like me anymore, not with my new black look, but it was best to keep my head down, just in case. I was also puzzled by the phone number underneath my picture: it didn't seem to be the usual anti-crime number, and I wondered if Oriana de la Force or Vulkan Sligo were running their own publicity campaign to find me.

A middle-aged guy in jeans and a striped T-shirt was the only other person waiting in the shelter. I didn't like the way he kept looking at me, and I was relieved when my bus arrived. As we pulled out, I glanced back at him, still sitting on the bench, talking on his phone. I turned away and put him, with so many other paranoid thoughts, to the back of my mind.

8:13 pm

It was pretty dark by the time I got off at the Long Reef stop and walked the few hundred yards or so towards the cluster of buildings I could see down the road. Even though the streetlights were very dim, the large, white building I was looking for stood out clearly.

Labtech
Long Reef

8:27 pm

The Labtech government laboratories were set in bushland at the end of a long, winding road where I was met with a parking gate. I ducked beneath it and ran for cover in some bushes that lined the driveway on the other side.

I made my way up towards the reception entrance, noticing that the vast parking lot to the left of the building was, as Jennifer had predicted, empty. I was a little early, so I sat under the leafy cover for a while and kept watch.

8:52 pm

Nothing had moved in the last twenty minutes. I felt pretty sure that the grounds were deserted . . . aside from one particular person, waiting inside for her meeting with a teen fugitive.

I was so anxious to meet her and find out what she had for me.

I ran up to the entrance doors and pressed the red after-hours buzzer on my right. Shortly after, there was a buzzing sound and the lock was released. I pressed the heavy door open.

"Turn left after the reception desk," Jennifer's voice advised me through the intercom, "and follow the corridor all the way to the end. I'll be waiting there for you."

8:58 pm

I followed Jennifer's directions, past a number of doorways and offices, until I found her waiting by a window in a small central area, the hub from which a number of narrow corridors led off in different directions. I approached with caution.

She wore a white lab coat that looked big and bulky on her small figure, and a pale blue paper cap covered her light brown hair that was tied in the back in a small ponytail. She came towards me with a warm smile and a look of relief. I held my hand out to shake hers, but she ignored it and came right in for a hug.

I was completely taken by surprise by her affection, and for a moment I felt like I was reuniting with family. I was also surprised by how unafraid she was of me.

I felt a surge of relief — at last we'd met. She stepped back, and seemed to examine me. She had gentle eyes and pale skin, and she smelled of peppermint.

"Want one?" she asked, pulling a small tin of mints out from a fold in her lab coat.

"Thanks," I said, taking one.

"The stink of the solvents gets a bit much for me sometimes," she said, smiling.

Immediately, I liked her. I felt I could trust her.

"You're so much like Tom," she said, leading me down one of the corridors. "I nursed Tom up until, you know, we lost him."

I felt comforted hearing her say my dad's name.

We turned off the corridor into a small laboratory and Jennifer hastily closed the door behind us. "He was a very special patient to all of the people who nursed him," she said, "especially me. We all wanted him to recover.

But he steadily got worse. Cal, he wasn't crazy. He just lost his connectors. Everything got mixed up in his mind. He worked so hard on those drawings for you. Tell me, do you have them?"

"Yes," I said, hoping I was wise to trust her. Thinking about Dad made me so sad, but it was good to be talking to someone else who had valued him. It made me feel more determined than ever that I was going to solve the mystery he'd left me. "Thanks," I said. "I haven't had anyone around to talk to about Dad for a while . . . You must know the amount of trouble I'm in?"

"Of course I do."

"And you're not scared of me?"

"No," she said, like it didn't need explaining.

I slowly followed her around the laboratory, checking it out. "What sort of work do you do here?" I asked, intrigued by all the strange-looking lab equipment.

"We make vaccines in one section, but this area is for antivenom production. You might notice a lot of information about reptiles around the place; we keep a lot of snakes here, very venomous ones. We milk the snakes then process their venom into the antidotes to their own toxins."

Great, I thought, now noticing all the snake-related posters and charts crowding the walls. Just what I need . . . more dangerous animals.

As we walked along together, she pointed out a closed door a little further along the corridor. "This is where we keep our stores of antivenom."

She opened the door, and I looked through. A row of small fridges ran along one side of the room. After she switched the light on, I saw that each fridge was labeled with the name of a deadly snake: brown snake, krait, desert viper, death adder, coral snake.

She closed the door again.

"So you said you've got your father's drawings?" she asked.

I was immediately suspicious again. Why did she want to know that?

"The drawings are safe," I said, knowing they were right there behind me, in their folder in the lining of my backpack.

"Tom was very concerned about those drawings. He wanted you to have them. The doctors would happily have sent them to your mother or your uncle, but I knew it was you he wanted them sent to, so I made sure that happened."

"Thanks," I said.

"I have something else for you that your father wanted to give you . . . but, Cal," she paused and took my hand, "I'm afraid I haven't got it here for you tonight."

"What do you mean?" I asked, pulling my hand back. "What is it? Why did you make me come here then?"

"Look, I don't want to alarm you — and you'll probably think I'm completely paranoid — but I had a bad feeling this morning that someone was hanging around my apartment. Now I didn't even see anyone, or anything," she said, shaking her hands and her head simultaneously to stress her point, "it was just a feeling. Probably nothing."

"What do you mean, *feeling*?"

"You know that feeling you get when you know someone's watching you, even though you have your back to them?"

I know it all too well, I thought to myself.

"It was kind of like that . . ." she continued. "I think I probably also felt a little anxious about finally meeting you, so maybe it was nothing at all . . . Regardless," she said, "it was enough to make me leave the memory stick behind."

"A memory stick? What was on it?"

"Back in the hospice, when your dad was pretty far along in his illness," she sighed, "I was clearing out some of his stuff from his toiletry bag when the memory stick fell out. He could barely move, but I sensed in his eyes, from his bed, he was trying to tell me that it contained something very important. I'd been experimenting and trying out different techniques of communicating with him, so I held it up and asked him, 'What's this?' and 'Who is it for?' Immediately he began trying to point with his eyes to a photograph — the one of you two at the airfield. I said to him, 'Tom, it's OK. I'll give it to Cal, I promise,' and I could see the rush of relief calm his body."

I felt a strange mixture of sorrow and joy to hear this.

"Do you know what's on it?"

"Yes, I had a look. My guess is that they're photographs from Ireland. There are lots of green fields and ruins. I have no idea how they could be important, but maybe you will." She stood a moment listening to something, then went back to the lab door.

"Did you hear something?" she asked.

"What?"

"There it is again!"

I came to the door to join her and listened intently. "What did it sound like?" I asked.

"I thought I heard footsteps — down the hallway."

All I could pick up was the low hum of the air-conditioning, and the sound of distant traffic from the main road up the hill.

"Are you sure the door locked after you came in?" she asked.

I thought for a second. "I'm pretty sure I heard it click behind me. It's a heavy, air-pressured door, isn't it? Not the kind you need to close after you."

"You're right. It must have been one of the lab animals," Jennifer said, rushing a couple of feet away to peer through a narrow window, high in the wall. I looked around, but I couldn't see any lab animals, let alone hear any. I was worried. I didn't know any animals that could make sounds like human footsteps. Especially not snakes.

Could someone have followed *me* here after all? I recalled the librarians at Liberty Square and how they'd been whispering together. If they'd reported my location to the authorities, cops could have been watching the surrounding places like bus stops and train stations. I thought of the man in the striped T-shirt at the bus shelter. Had he recognized me and called someone? Was he on the phone to the authorities as we pulled away from the curb?

9:39 pm

"I'd better start locking up now," Jennifer said, taking a set of keys from a drawer. "If you want to come and do the rounds with me, I can tell you what I know, and we can find a way to get the memory stick safely to you."

I followed her down the building as she checked doors and switched off lights. We seemed to be the only people around, but I wondered why a building that size didn't have security.

"Where are your security people?" I asked her.

"Patrolling the grounds out back somewhere," she said. "This is a huge complex. They'll probably be back up this way around eleven."

9:45 pm

"Cal," she said, as we continued through the maze of corridors and corners, "I don't mean to scare you again, but your father was very worried about someone towards the end of his life. Someone other than himself," she clarified.

"Who?"

"I never found out. He couldn't speak at that stage, and I hadn't managed to find just the right way of getting information out of him. He had been able to manage a few words earlier when he'd asked another nurse to get a book for him — *Treasure Island* by Robert Louis Stevenson, but that was before I began working closely with him. This other nurse thought it was a strange choice, but she found a copy and gave it to him. Instead of being pleased, he just threw it on the floor. She said he seemed utterly despairing, frustrated that she'd failed to correctly interpret his words. She knew he was desperate to communicate something — but he just couldn't make it happen in a way she understood."

"What was that?" I asked, hearing an odd noise.

"Could be the door of my office," said Jennifer, hurrying along ahead of me and vanishing around a corner.

"Wait up," I said, following her.

But just before turning the corner, my attention was caught by a glass enclosure lower down in the wall, and I stopped for a moment to see what was in it. Within seconds, a brown snake swiftly untangled its coils. Despite glass between us, I jumped back in fright as the snake struck. Two white fangs scraped the glass. Drops of venom slowly trickled down on the other side of the glass.

I backed away and hurried along, trying to

catch up with Jennifer.

I couldn't see her anywhere. Where had she gone? Why did I let myself get distracted when I was supposed to be following her in this warren of corridors? I muttered to myself.

"Jennifer?" I called out.

She didn't answer. The corridor she'd turned down branched off into two different directions. "Jennifer?" I called, this time louder.

Why wasn't she answering me? I recalled the noise we'd heard earlier. I had the feeling we were not alone in this building anymore — and I didn't think it was the security guards.

I hurried down the left wing, calling her name again.

Still no answer. I didn't know what to do.

"Jennifer?" I called again, louder still, backtracking and checking the right-hand corridor, trying to remember where her office was located.

Lights went out in the distance.

"Who's there?" I called.

By now I was freaking out. I would never be able to find my way out without Jennifer's help. Plus, I was really worried about what had happened to her. Had I put yet another person, who was trying to help me, in danger?

I stopped, wondering what to do next, when

I was frozen with fear. At the other end of the corridor, a figure suddenly ducked behind the wall. Despite the speed of the person's movement, I'd seen the distinct red tank top that I'd come to know and dread so well. Why couldn't he get a life . . . and some new clothes?

How on earth could *he* be here? Somehow, he'd followed me. Maybe the guy in the striped top at the bus shelter had been one of Sligo's spies . . .

Silently, I started backing away. If I could just get to the corner, I could take off and run with all I've got and he'd have no idea which branch of the T-junction I'd taken.

When I was almost at the junction I turned — and ran straight into another thug! Sligo had sent two of his troops out after me!

I didn't have time to be frightened. I didn't have time to think how all this was possible. All I could think of was getting away.

The man grabbed me and flipped me around so that my back was to him. The jolt really killed my leg, and the pain made me furious. I kicked backwards with my good leg, using all my strength, and my heel smashed into his shin. He hadn't seen that coming, and he howled in pain, loosening his grip just enough for me to twist away from him and barrel straight into Red Tank Top who'd appeared from another corridor. Without even thinking, I punched out hard between his legs! He screamed and doubled over, and I was away!

10:11 pm

I ran like crazy, I didn't know where — I just ran and ran and ran, up and down corridors, up and down flights of stairs, but after a few minutes of thinking I was free of them, the sounds of their thundering feet and shouts returned. I kept running, trying to block out their menacing threats of what they were going to do to me when they caught me.

Their thudding feet skidded closer and closer, and I realized I was headed for a dead end!

But there *was* a door! If it was locked, I was a goner. There was nowhere else to go except straight through it. I didn't even slow down, I just charged at it and thankfully the door flew open wide. I raced inside, kicking the door closed again behind me.

I'd have to find another way out — a window, a vent, a fire escape, anything. But it was as black as night in there. While fumbling in the dark for the light switch, I tripped over a metal trashcan and crashed straight into something hard. Glass shattered and smashed all over the floor around me, as loud as a torrential hailstorm. The pain of the impact on my side shot right through me.

Breathless and probably bleeding, I found the light switch . . .

To my absolute horror, I saw that I'd smashed open one of the cases — a glass case housing snakes! The floor was alive with them!

The label lay crooked on a shard of glass on the floor: death adders.

Two things happened simultaneously: the lights flashed on and off overhead, and, from somewhere in the building, a piercing alarm sounded. The writhing mass of brown serpents seemed to swarm to me. I froze, not knowing what to do . . . One snake came dangerously close to my foot . . . and then it happened . . . it reared up and struck at my jeans.

10:20 pm

I had to get out of there! I knew that death adders were about the most venomous snakes in the world, and the room I was standing in was alive with them. After the lion attack at the zoo, and now this, I was convinced the vicious world of nature had it in for me.

The internal alarm continued to blare through the building, and I ran across the slithering beasts and back to the door, flinging it open. Security would be here any minute. I'd pick security and even Sligo's thugs over a room full of death adders any day.

I hoped that the fangs hadn't penetrated through my jeans and into my skin, and that the sound of the alarm had scared off Sligo's men. I couldn't feel anything strange yet, but the alarm had done nothing to scare my enemies — at the other end of the corridor, the two thugs were heading straight for me!

10:21 pm

I looked around in despair. Behind me, the snakes. Ahead of me, Sligo's thugs. I had nowhere to go.

The two thugs suddenly stopped and I saw looks of horror on their faces.

Death adders, excited by the lights in the corridors, slithered with devastating speed right past me and straight for my attackers!

For once things were going my way. The thugs turned and ran, while I desperately backtracked and looked around for somewhere to hide.

10:25 pm

I was hiding in the dark under a sink in a small bathroom not far from the snake room. The security team had arrived, and they were checking doors and talking on their portable radios. At one stage, the door to the bathroom was opened and someone waved a flashlight around, but luckily they withdrew, satisfied with their minimal efforts to investigate the disturbance.

I waited anxiously for time to pass so I could move on.

Everything had been quiet for a while. It was time for me to come out of my hiding place and try to get out of this maze of corridors and levels.

Silently, I climbed out and crept to the bathroom door. I peered out into the moonlit corridor, and right at that moment, a blinding headache hit me. It was so strong and so violent that I fell against the wall. It wasn't just a headache — my eyes felt pierced by splinters of light that came from somewhere inside my own head. And there was a weakness in my legs that I couldn't understand.

A powerful nausea doubled me over. Pain throbbed in both of my legs.

Dreading what I might find, I rolled up my jeans.

Two tiny red wounds on the side of my calf, left by the death adder's fangs, oozed pinkish fluid.

10:34 pm

I staggered from door to door, trying to find the room that Jennifer had earlier shown me, with its row of fridges and its store of antivenom. Half-blind from the headache, and doubled over by the waves of sickening nausea, I fought on and continued stumbling from room to room.

Nothing.

If I didn't find it quickly, I knew I'd have to call an ambulance and that would end in my arrest, and the last chance to fulfill my father's wishes would be gone. I couldn't let that happen.

I had to find that corridor — all I could remember was that it was somewhere near the entrance area. But with a blazing headache and the blinding pain in my eyes, it was becoming more and more difficult to stay focused.

10:45 pm

My heart was thumping behind my ribs. Muscles in my leg went into spasm. It was getting hard to breathe; I had to pull air into my lungs. I stood swaying in the hallway, knowing that I had to get help. I could feel the stiffening of the muscles in my neck. If I didn't make a decision soon, I would be paralyzed, unable to breathe and then it would be too late.

10:48 pm

I just made it back to the reception area and somehow, through my blurring vision, I found the corridor we had walked down together. Strangely, the door was slightly ajar.

I practically fell into the room. Leaning heavily against the wall, I switched on the light. The pain in my eyes was almost unbearable. Moving like an old man, I groped my way along the fridges until I came to the one labeled *Death Adder Antivenom*. I pulled the door open, trying to focus. The stiffness in my neck was getting worse — I could barely move my head. My swaying arm knocked several boxes out of the fridge. I grabbed one and tore at the box, ripping it open.

The pre-loaded syringes tumbled out, and I managed to roll up my sleeve, stab the needle and depress the plunger. It stung like anything. I slid to the floor.

11:47 pm

I tried to sit up. I didn't know where I was or what had happened for a few seconds, but then things started coming back to me, and I realized I'd passed out. Both my legs were hurting, but the blinding headache had gone and my vision seemed to be almost normal again. There was no more stiffness in my neck, and I no longer felt like throwing up. Slowly I got to my feet. I swayed a little, but I stayed upright.

The antivenom had worked. The alarms had stopped ringing, but what had happened to security?

11:49 pm

A groaning sound in the furthest corner of the laboratory made me jump. I was about to try and bolt, when a second low moan made me realize it was a woman. Jennifer! Cautiously, I went over to find her lying half hidden by a pile of cartons.

I knelt down beside her, helping her sit up.

"What happened?" she asked me, groggily.

"I don't know," I said. "Some people are after me — they must have trailed me here."

"Oww," she cried, grabbing the back of her head.

"Here, let me have a look."

She winced in pain as I moved her forward so I could check for an injury.

Blood was soaking her hair, and she had an ugly cut on her scalp. She couldn't have faked that. Someone had hit her, for sure.

"Someone must have hit you from behind, then dragged you in here," I said, still a little unsure.

She put her hand on the back of her head and winced in pain. "Great security we've got," she said bitterly. "They do nothing but strut around. This is the last straw!"

"Umm," I said, about to mention the glass case I'd accidentally smashed. "They might have seen something that made them run away . . ."

Jennifer wasn't listening. "Cal, what about you? Are you all right?" she asked in a rush.

"I'm OK," I said, glancing at the list of emergency phone numbers on the wall and picking up the phone to make the call, "but you were hit on the head. You could have a concussion."

"Who are they?" she asked, ignoring my concern. "Those people that came after us?"

"People who are after the information Dad left me. They were after *me*," I said. "You just got in their way."

"So it wasn't anyone that had followed *me*?"

"No, these guys have been on my tail for some time now," I said, thinking that it felt like they'd always been after me. "But you should definitely stay on your guard, too, I'm afraid."

The emergency operator answered my call. I told him that we needed an ambulance and that there was someone with a head injury. As soon as I'd given him the details of our location, I hung the phone up — I needed to get out of there before the paramedics arrived.

Jennifer stood up slowly and made her way to a chair. I poured her a glass of water in a paper cup.

"Cal," she said, "I understand that you have to go . . . but I need you to know that your father was very troubled about something. I didn't realize just how serious it was, or how dangerous . . . until now. It's *big*. You must be very, very careful. Please say you will be?"

I knew it all too well. "I'll do my best," I said, pulling my bag back on, "But when do you think you can give me the memory stick?"

"I'll call you. Soon, OK?"

In the distance, I could hear the ambulance approaching.

I nodded. "You can't really blame security for getting out of here like they did."

Jennifer looked puzzled.

"Here," I said, handing her the phone from the nearby desk. "Keep that door closed. You'd better get the snake catchers in," I added. "The death adders escaped."

19 MARCH

288 days to go . . .

12:10 am

I walked into the night happy to be alive, and free, for the moment, from all of my pursuers. I made my way from the Labtech complex through the bushes alongside the road, and was relieved to see the ambulance zoom past me on its way to Jennifer.

The climb back up the hill was rough, but once I made it to the top I could see the twinkling lights of the city below, and I was grateful that the walk home was pretty much downhill.

Hideout
38 St. Johns Street

10:58 am

It had been a long walk home — if you could call a derelict house a *home* — and I'd crashed almost the second I'd climbed back inside.

My head was spinning when I woke up and thought about everything that had happened in the laboratories. I pulled out my phone, keen to tell Boges about it.

"Hey, Robbo," Boges answered, clearly not alone. "What's happening? How's the studying going?"

I got it right away. "You can't talk. Your mum's there?"

"Right, right."

"Do you have a couple of minutes to listen?" I asked, hoping for that, at least.

"Sure I do, Robbo! Yeah, go ahead."

I quickly told him about meeting Jennifer Smith at Labtech in Long Reef, and how she'd hoped to give me Dad's memory stick but wasn't able to last night. I then went on to sum up the messy encounter with Red Tank Top and his thug friend . . . and then finally the death adder bite and the fridge of antivenom. I said it as fast and in as few words as possible.

The other end of the line was quiet for a moment. I could tell Boges was working out what he could say without raising suspicion.

"What's next? Crocodiles?" he finally said, laughing a little awkwardly.

"Tell me about it," I sighed. "It was so bad. My head felt like it was going to explode, and I just wanted to throw up. But the antivenom seemed to work perfectly. Sure, I felt pretty groggy afterwards, and still do, but that was nothing compared to possibly having that slithery sucker take me down! Imagine that, after everything I've been through."

"No kidding!" said Boges. "It was a good thing she didn't bring it," he added.

"Jennifer? The memory stick?"

"Exactly."

"Because of Sligo's thugs?"

"Exactly," Boges agreed.

"Hey, I called Eric Blair again, and guess what?"

"Go on."

"He's still off on sick leave," I said. "Can you believe it? What do you think's wrong with him?

"OK, you can't really answer that, can you," I said, after nothing but silence on Boges's end of the line. "Anyway, we'll talk about it later."

"Listen, Rob, I'm sorry mate," said Boges, "but I have to get going. Can I call you back in the next day or two?"

"That'd be great."

"Cool," he said. "In the meantime, I'll see if I can dig up some information on snakes for

your class project — venom, snake-bite care —
I've done a few reptile studies which could help
you out with getting back into Mr. Lloyd's good
books."

"You're awesome, Boges, thanks."

21 MARCH
286 days to go . . .

3:57 pm

"Dude, I am so sorry I haven't been able to call you back until now. That phone call the other day was rough! Mum and Gran kept coming in and out of my room so I could hardly say a word! I can't believe you were bitten by a death adder! Is everything OK now?" Boges asked me.

"That's cool, don't worry about it. Yeah, everything seems fine. I feel fine," I assured him.

Boges went on for a while, sounding like a medical dictionary. Basically he was telling me that I had to rest up, keep the wound clean, and be on the lookout for any deterioration.

"What do you mean by deterioration?" I asked.

"There's this thing called tissue necrosis. It's when the skin dies and goes black. You haven't got any blackness happening, do you? Any oozing?"

"No, nothing."

"What about suppurating pustules?"

"Sounds disgusting. What are they?"

"Kind of like massive zits. I saw some pictures of them online. Talk about gruesome!"

"No, nothing like that," I said, relieved.

"Just as well you weren't bitten by a giant Amazonian Swamp Viper," said Boges. "In two days, the bitten limb turns green, then black, then drops off entirely."

"Lucky me!" I said sarcastically. "And how about Eric Blair?" I added.

"That's very strange," said Boges.

"Tell me about it," I agreed. "Anyway, I'd better let you go. Thanks heaps for that info. Text me when you can come around again, OK, and we can talk about getting into Oriana's?"

"For sure."

4:38 pm

I changed the dressing on the old wound on my other leg, adding more antiseptic and changing the bandages. It had healed pretty well, and almost all of Repro's tiny stitches had fallen out.

Next, I washed the swollen area around the snake-bite, the cold water cooling the inflamed skin. I shook my head, thinking about being bitten by a giant Amazonian Swamp Viper.

I definitely needed to stay away from all dangerous creatures.

25 MARCH

282 days to go . . .

9:15 am

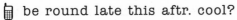 be round late this aftr. cool?
📱 sweet. thx boges. c u then.

5:03 pm

It was a cool afternoon, and the sun was hidden behind the overgrown trees in the backyard of the old house where I was sitting, reading a book I'd taken from Repro's.

A couple of days earlier, two men in suits had come to the door with clipboards and I'd hidden under the house while they made notes about the property. I guessed they were people who were considering buying and developing the land occupied by the old house. That worried me. If I was right, and they were starting their demolition plans, I'd have to find another place to live. This place was far from being a palace, but it had a working toilet and a sink with the water still on.

As the days passed, I wondered why Jennifer hadn't called me and hoped she wasn't in the hospital. Thinking of the hospital made me think of Gabbi, and I pulled out my phone to look at the photo of her that Boges had sent me. It made me sad, but I couldn't help staring at it.

I'd been out late at night and scrounged some more furniture from the thrown-outs along the nearby streets. Now I had another table set up on bricks that I'd scavenged from a building site, and a couple of old cushiony chairs. For some days I'd had the drawings up on the walls, and it had been comforting to have Dad's work all around me. They weren't up for long before I took them down again, worried that if I had to make a hasty exit I wouldn't be able to collect them in time.

I kept my mind busy with my book as I waited for Boges to show up, when a sound around the front of the house made me freeze.

These days Boges always arrived by tunneling under the house. Always. This sounded as if someone was coming up to the front door, and I feared that the clipboard men were back.

I put my book down, crept back inside, and peered through the crack near the front door, ready to dive down the hole in the floorboards.

It was the sound of tiny bells that made me realize who it was. That, and a whiff of a familiar perfume that sent my mind spinning.

How had Winter Frey found out where I was?

I waited, trying to work out how she might have done it, but my thoughts were quickly interrupted.

"Cal? Cal, I know you're in there. I need to talk to you. You're in danger."

I knew that already — I didn't need Winter Frey telling me that again.

"Stop pretending you're not there! Let me in!"

Somehow, she'd found out where I was staying. Things couldn't get any worse if I let her in.

"I know you must think I set you up, but I didn't, I swear!"

She started thumping on the door. "Cal," she shouted, "let me in!"

"Hey, shut up will you? I'm trying to hide in here!" I said through the crack.

"You *are* there!" she cried, just as loud, running over to the crack I had spoken through. She ducked down, peering an eye through, and whispered, "Please, Cal, let me in. I promise I did not set you up. I was trying to warn you that they were trailing you and weren't far away. You've got to believe me. Besides," she added, "it'd be too late now for you to get away if I was working for them."

"How did you track me down?" I asked. Her eye looked huge surrounded by smoky gray eye shadow.

"It'd be a lot easier to talk to you if you'd just let me in."

I gave in and quickly opened the front door for her.

"It was simple," she said, walking right into the main room, but before she could tell me any more, a sound from under the floor caused us both to swing around. I thought it would be Boges, but still made sure that I had a clear run through to the back door just in case it wasn't. I had an exit plan worked out — over the back fence and away.

"What's that noise under the floor?" Winter asked.

She looked even more surprised when the carpet in the middle of the room went flying, and Boges's head and shoulders appeared through the hole in the floor like an oversized meerkat.

"You!" said Boges, halfway through the floorboards, staring at Winter.

"Yes, *me*," Winter snapped back. "So?"

I looked from one to the other as they glared at each other.

Slowly, Boges hauled himself up out of the hole.

"You're the girl that's been hanging around my place! Hard to miss someone with eyes like yours. And, you know," Boges added, "people put bells on their cats so that birds can *hear* them coming. It's not a very clever move for someone who's trying to *sneak* around to wear bells on their skirt!" Boges swiveled his hips like a belly dancer. "People can hear you a mile away!"

Winter gave me a look as if to say *you'd better shut your friend up*, then pulled a newspaper clipping out of her bag. "And you can't be missed either, clever boy," she said, waving it at Boges.

"Best friend knows nothing of teen disappearance." I read from beneath a grainy picture of Boges standing outside his house on Dorothy Road.

"It wasn't hard to find out where you lived," she said, raising her right eyebrow, revealing, even more so, the intensity of her dark eyes. "I recognized your house from this picture. I've also noticed Zombrovski watching your place. Bruno's been looking for you too," she turned to me, "all over the city."

"Bruno?" I asked. "Who's Bruno?"

"One of Sligo's men. This big dude who

fancies himself a top street fighter. He always wears this stupid red tank top."

"He nearly got me at a government laboratory," I interrupted, "but the snakes got me instead."

"Snakes?" Her eyes widened.

"Another time," I said. "Tell me more about Bruno. Why is he always wearing that same stupid tank top?"

"Bruno's high up in Sligo's gang. I can't stand him. He got the tank top from a Chinese martial arts guy, thinking that the characters on the tank top mean *Master Fighter*," she laughed, "but I know what they really mean . . ."

"And what's that?" I asked.

Winter shook her head. "I'll tell you some other time. Maybe. Anyway, both Bruno and Zombrovski missed you because they're both stupid, but I'm not. I just followed *your friend* the other day — all the way here," she said, turning to Boges, "I watched you look around, then creep in here up the side, thinking you were all sneaky and stuff . . . I knew who you were visiting." She put her hands on her hips, cocking her head to one side. "You're not really that smart at all," she said. "You led me straight to the kid every cop in the state is trying to catch."

"Give me that!" said Boges, trying to snatch the newspaper from her. Winter was quick, and easily pulled it out of his reach. She shoved it back in her pocket.

"So I guess I don't have to introduce you two then," I said.

"Nope. You're Winter Frey all right," said Boges, and he didn't sound too friendly. "At first I thought you were a thief, hanging around my place waiting to steal my wallet."

"Your wallet! That's a joke. I don't need your money."

Stand off, I thought.

"Anyway, Winter," I interrupted. "How come you just appear and disappear like some sort of optical illusion?"

"I don't have to give an account of myself to you. Who do you think you are?"

"There's no mystery about me," I said. "You know exactly who I am."

"And that's what I'm afraid of, dude," said Boges. "This chick knows far too much. What's she doing here, anyway? Didn't you say she gave you to Sligo? Isn't that how you ended up almost sliced-and-diced on the train tracks?"

Winter looked shocked, and a little wounded, by what Boges had just said. "Sliced-and-diced?" she repeated, softly.

"Yeah, you little rat, you nearly got him killed," Boges shouted at her.

"Stop it! Both of you!" I said, standing between the fiery pair. My head couldn't deal with them fighting just then. "I've got enough stuff going on. I don't need this."

They both backed off and looked away.

"Thank you," I said.

Boges looked up strangely at me, all of a sudden.

"What?" I asked him.

"Dude, what's with your hair?!" he asked, before bursting into a fit of laughter. I couldn't believe it! I looked at Winter, and she'd started laughing too!

I could feel my face flush red with embarrassment, and my hands flew up to my hair, trying to do something with it to make it look less flat.

"He looks ridiculous!" she laughed.

"Totally!" Boges agreed.

If laughing at me put an end to their fighting, then I'd have to accept it. Besides, I knew that my new black, combed-down 'do did look pretty bad.

5:55 pm

With the jokes about my hair finally over, we all

went out to the back porch and sat next to each other with our legs dangling off the edge.

I turned to Boges. "What's the latest on Mum and Gabbi?"

Boges wouldn't look at me. "Same as last time," he said.

I was aware of a gentle hand on my shoulder and looked beside me, surprised. Winter whipped her hand away as if she'd been burned. For a moment our eyes met, until she picked up her skirt, stood up and walked away.

I thought she'd left, but then I saw her huddled down on the side of the porch, a little way off.

6:12 pm

Boges had brought some rolls and cold meat with him, and we threw them together and started eating. Winter sat quietly at the other end of the porch, some distance away from us, fiddling with the bells on the bottom of her skirt.

Boges and Winter had not gotten off to a good start, I thought. She was a difficult girl, no question. But she'd put her hand on my shoulder as if to comfort me. I found myself staring at her when she wasn't looking . . .

6:18 pm

"It's only a matter of time," said Winter, breaking the silence and looking up from where she was sitting, "before Sligo finds out where you are."

"If you haven't told him already," said Boges.

"I'll ignore that," she said crisply, wiping her hands on her skirt. "Stupidity is so unattractive."

"Why," I asked, "are you interested in helping me? I still don't get it."

Winter gave me a sharp look. "You don't have to get it," she said.

She got up again and stalked away, pushing branches out of the way, disappearing into the overgrowth. I could see her pop up occasionally, picking the purple and yellow flowers from the vine that grew all over the backyard. Boges sat down again beside me on the step of the sagging back porch. He glanced in Winter's direction.

"Cal," he said, lowering his voice, "there's something you should know. Your mum told me that your uncle has hired a private detective to find you. She said he is determined to track you down — bring you home again. He wants you all to be together again as a family, and he said he doesn't care how much it costs him. He said he'll stand beside you and support you and get you the help you need."

"The only help I need is to discover the truth about the Ormond Singularity," I said, dreading the thought of having yet another person following me. "And stop the criminals who are trying to destroy me and cash in on my dad's secret. If I can do that, I won't need any help clearing my name. Everyone will see that I didn't hurt Gabbi or my uncle."

Boges grunted. "OK. So what's the grand plan?" he asked. "We've gotta get hold of that paper on Oriana de la Force's desk, right? How do you think we're going to get in there?"

I had counted on Boges's help, but had changed my mind about it just this morning. I could see he wanted to help me out, and I didn't want to hurt his feelings, but I knew that he was not the man for this sort of job. Boges wasn't a fighter. He was the brains of this operation. Plus I didn't want to put my friend in any more danger. What I needed was someone with Singapore martial arts championship experience under their belt.

"I've got something slightly different planned now," I said to Boges. "If Oriana found out that you'd been in her house, or taken something from her, you'd be joining me on the run. I've heard a few stories about her — about what happens to people who cross her, and as much as I'd love to have you around . . ."

"That's OK," agreed Boges, a little too quickly. "You know I'm up for it, if you change your mind."

Winter appeared holding several of the purple and yellow flowers from the vine. Against the dark green garden and soft light, she stood out like a rainbow.

She came up the stairs and sat beside me. "You don't look very happy," she said, as her skirt made a sinking cloud around her.

"I've never been happier in my life," I said. "I've got the police, and now a private detective, two criminal gangs including your Mr. Sligo —"

"— he's not *my* Mr. Sligo!" she snapped.

Boges's face was a picture of disbelief. "You hang around with him, though," he said. "Maybe Cal got that the wrong way around. Maybe he's not *your* Mr. Sligo. But maybe you're *his* girl!"

Winter jumped to her feet, her eyes blazing with anger. "You don't know anything about me!" she cried. "You should just shut your big mouth!"

She ran inside the house, and I jumped up after her, following her inside.

"Hey! Put that down!" I yelled, when I saw her pick up my backpack.

Instead, she stood there, one hand on her hip, the other holding out my backpack. "Seeing as how your so-called best friend hasn't got the brains to warn you, *I'll* have to do it. You *have* to believe what I've been trying to tell you!" she said. "You *must* leave this place!"

I frowned. "Do you know something I don't?"

"I heard them talking the other night. I heard Sligo saying he knows what area of the city you live in now. That he's narrowed it down. You don't have time to be sitting around. You need to *move*."

I thought of how Red Tank Top — Bruno — and his companion had been able to follow me to the laboratory where Jennifer worked. It did feel as if Sligo was closing in on me.

"So put this on," Winter threw my bag to me, "and get moving. Don't you see?" Winter continued, "If *I* could track *him* here," she looked at Boges, who'd just walked inside to join us, "anyone could. It's just a matter of time before either Vulkan Sligo or the authorities find out where you are."

Boges nodded. "She's right," he said, but his face narrowed. I could see he hated to admit that. And I knew he was trying to work out what her angle was in this. Just like I was.

Out of nowhere, the sound of a tremendous crash had us all scrambling to our feet. I watched transfixed, as the old front door fell flat on the ground, and a wild and disheveled woman, wearing filthy clothing and clutching a shiny black suitcase, fell into the house on top of the door. She scrambled to her feet, gestured back over her shoulder and shrieked, "They're after me! They're after me!" then continued her wild race through the house, disappearing out the back door.

The sounds of her scrambling outside through the overgrown garden and over the back fence thrashed through our ears. Then we all saw the reason for the woman's flight. A huge cop, wearing riot gear, filled the door frame. And he was intent on pursuing his catch.

6:48 pm

"Where's that filthy thief?" his voice boomed, as he ran through the house after the wild woman. Winter made a dash to the back door as I tried to run through the door the cop had just come through . . . and then I heard Boges shout.

I turned sharply to see that the riot cop had a partner, who'd come up the side of the house. He had Boges. And before I knew what was happening, he'd grabbed me too.

"All right," he snarled, "I want to see some sort of identification."

I couldn't even move under the cop's iron grip.

"Sure thing, officer," said Boges, searching his pockets with his free hand. "It was here a minute ago," he muttered. "I always carry my bus pass with me."

The big cop turned his attention to me. "And what about you? I don't like the look of you at all." He peered more closely at my face. "Don't I know you?"

"No way," I said. "I've just got that sort of face. People think they know it."

"Don't be smart with me, pal."

"I wasn't being smart, I was —"

"Quiet!"

Boges couldn't find his bus pass, and I had nothing at all to show. I thought back to the passes I'd taken from Repro's, but there was no way I could pull one of them out now without the cop seeing my stash. I had to get out of this situation, but I couldn't think of how.

"OK. Both of you are coming along with me. I'm taking you down to the station. On suspicion."

"Suspicion of what?" Boges asked.

"On suspicion of being a serious smart mouth, that's what."

Boges gave me the look that he would give me when he was about to pass me a ball in soccer — he was about to make a run for it. But how was I going to get away?

Boges took off, attempting to run out the back door just like Winter had, but because he was bulkier, he was unable to disappear like she had. The cop took off after Boges, releasing his grip on me.

I'd just dropped into the hole in the floorboards when I saw Boges trip on a rotting floorboard and crash to the floor. The big cop collided with his body, and tripped over, falling on top of my friend.

They both flailed around, trying to get to their feet, when I spotted the cop's pepper spray, buttoned down on the back of his belt. His big backside, sticking up in the air as he finally pinned Boges down, gave me a great idea. I pulled myself back up into the room.

Quick as a flash, I grabbed my backpack, pulled out a tranquilizer syringe and ripped off the plastic seal. This was my chance! I had no idea where the other cop was and hoped he was a long way away by now, still chasing the thief.

I plunged the tranquilizer into the cop's uniformed backside. He roared, half stood up, swayed, then fell sideways, crashing heavily down onto the floor.

Boges slid out from under him, staring from the cop to me then back again, his eyes rounder than I'd ever seen them. "Awesome move, dude! Just awesome!"

"Quick!" I said. "Let's go. If his partner comes back we're totally screwed!"

The cop was out cold, the needle still in his backside, sticking up in the air. I leaned over him and pulled out his pepper spray.

From outside came the yells of the crazy woman. I could hear the first cop, who was now holding her, cursing as he dragged his prisoner away down the road. Any moment now, he'd be back to check up on his partner.

We had to get going.

"You better take that out," said Boges, pointing to the tranquilizer. "Fingerprints. DNA."

I did as he said, pushing the used syringe back into its lid and packing, stuffing it into my backpack.

"Now let's get out of here!" I grabbed Boges and my backpack, and we launched ourselves outside, keeping low until Boges cautiously took a look up and down the street.

"Looks OK. The cop car's parked down the

road a bit. Let's make a break for it!"

We ran as hard as we could, away from the police car and away from the house.

I didn't even have time to wonder what had happened to Winter Frey.

Unfamiliar street

10:20 pm

Boges had long gone home. Now I huddled in a doorway, far away in a small alley on the western side of the city, trying to rest for a moment and figure out where to go.

I was in big trouble. I knew that cop would never forget me or forgive me for taking him down, and I hoped that he'd be transferred to another part of the country, or another assignment — anything to get him off my back. Stealing police equipment was most likely a serious crime, too. But in my position, I had to grab whatever opportunities came my way. I was running for my life. Anything I could use to help me survive, I was going to take — even if I did have to take it from a cop.

I'd stowed the pepper spray in my backpack but I knew I had to find a safer place for it, and for the rest of my arsenal — the explosive detonator caps were in there too.

I heard the sounds of an argument coming from a building across from where I hunched. Curious, I snuck over and, through the open doorway, saw two men arguing over a card game. A bald-headed guy was already out of his seat and, as I watched, the other card player, a big skinhead in a leather jacket, jumped to his feet, knocking his chair right over. With a roar, the big bald-headed guy dived across the table, and within seconds the two of them were grappling with each other. The table tipped over, and the two men crashed to the floor, locked together.

I wasn't looking at them for long . . . I was focused on the pile of money that went flying from the tabletop. Without even thinking, I rushed in, past the men who were trying to throttle each other on the floor, and I scooped up as much of the cash as I could grab. I was just going for the last handful when I looked up and saw a kid standing in the doorway, looking in at me.

Shock jolted through my body!

It was him! I mean, me!

I was staring at my double again! He stood there, in a shirt and trousers, looking like he'd just stepped out of the office.

I forgot the possible danger I was in from the two fighting men. Everything around me seemed to stand still.

"Hey!" I yelled, as the spell broke and I jumped up, heading in my double's direction. I saw the fear in his eyes, as he realized it was me again, just before he turned and raced away.

"I only want to talk to you!" I yelled, taking off after him. And just as well I did, because my voice had alerted the skinhead and his bald-headed mate.

I was already halfway down the street by then and around the corner by the time they started coming after me. I saw my double race down an alley and disappear. With the two angry men coming after me, it wasn't a good time for me to follow him down an alley without knowing what was at the end of it. I couldn't risk it, so I ran past the alley, stuffing cash deeper into my pockets, on the run again.

The yells of rage faded as I continued to run, my backpack bumping up and down like crazy. I wondered how much of an impact the detonators needed to set them off.

It wasn't long before I'd lost them. I pulled up, puffing and panting, doubled over, trying to catch my breath. Who *was* this guy who looked exactly the same as me? What was a kid dressed like a bank teller doing on the streets around this scummy area? And most importantly, why did he keep running away from me? He'd recognized me, even with this black hair . . .

Slowly, my heart rate slowed and my breathing became more normal. I counted the money, and when I was finished I gave a yell of triumph. Finally, with my hoodie pulled all the way up to hide my face, I set off in the direction of the train station.

26 MARCH

281 days to go . . .

Repro's Lair

12:15 am

I felt a bit stupid knocking on the back wall of an old filing cabinet, but it was dark and there was no one around in the disused railway yard. I didn't know if Repro would mind me banging on his front door just after midnight, but I had a deal to put to him.

Realizing that he wouldn't answer unless he knew who it was, I hissed through the crack, "Repro! It's me! Cal! I want to talk to you about a job."

There was a long silence. Maybe he wasn't there. Then I heard his voice.

"What sort of job?"

"Something that I think will interest you."

"Sure you haven't brought anyone else with you?"

"I'm alone," I said. I was jiggling with anxiety.

He had to let me in again.

"Can't you tell me through the door?"

"I've got a deal for you. I need help getting into a house, but there could be trouble. And you were a black belt master."

I heard him clearing his throat. "That's right. So I was."

"Please let me in," I begged. "I need to talk business with you."

There was a long silence.

"Hey," I said, "I've got money . . ."

After a moment, I heard him dragging away the heavy wooden chest from the other side.

The back of the cabinet revolved and Repro's thin face appeared. "Then come in, my boy. Why on earth didn't you say so in the first place?"

Inside the stone cellar, there seemed to be even more towers of stuff filling the space since I'd last been there. I ducked under the clothes line, dodged an unsteady pile of books, and placed a wad of money on the table. Repro quickly snatched it up.

"This is a job for a black belt," I said. "For the man who won the championship at Singapore."

"Look," he said, fanning the notes through his fingers, "about that championship. Like I said, I *almost* won it."

"That's right," I said. "So you came second, right?"

"Not exactly," he said.

"But you almost won it!" I repeated.

"I *almost* did. Except I didn't."

"I understand that," I said, getting impatient.

"I *almost* got to Singapore is what I meant."

I stared at him. "You mean you weren't even *in* Singapore?"

"I was on my way, but I missed my plane."

"But you said . . ." I started to say. "You weren't even there?"

Repro pushed his thin hair back from his high forehead. "I would have won the competition if I'd been in it!"

"Great," I said, anger making my voice sharp. "I'll take my money back, thanks!"

His narrow face crinkled into a laugh. "I'm a mean street fighter! Just give me a chance to show you what I can do. You won't be sorry!"

"I'm sorry already," I said.

"Come on," he said. "Give me a chance. Don't be like that."

"Money, please." I put out my hand.

Slowly he started to pass back the money. "If you give me a chance, you won't regret it. I'm fast on my feet, and a quick thinker in a tight spot."

He stopped for a second, just before the money hit my open hand, and looked at me. I looked back into his wide possum eyes and thought about the guardian angel pin he'd given me. My open hand closed.

"Here's the deal," I said. "Two hundred dollars all up. Half now, the other half once the job is done. And," I added, "you gotta let me crash here again tonight."

He shook my hand fervently with his bony fingers. "You've got it. I won't let you down."

30 MARCH

277 days to go . . .

Outside Oriana de la Force's house

6:13 pm

We'd been crouched in the bushes watching Oriana's house for a while. A few people had come and gone, and Oriana herself had left about half an hour ago in her dark blue Mercedes. She seemed to take one bodyguard with her, but I couldn't tell which one. She'd yelled out something into the house as she left, so we knew that there was still at least one person inside.

We didn't know how long it would be before she came back, so we needed to act fast.

I prepared to move. I reassured myself by feeling the pepper spray in the pocket of my hoodie, and by checking the clipboard with the flower delivery slip we'd prepared earlier. Between us sat a long, white box, held together with a red satin bow, and containing a dozen long-stemmed crimson roses.

I was wearing an outfit Repro and I had pulled together from the collection. I wore a black cap, a light gray, long-sleeved shirt, black trousers and a lanyard around my neck. I had even added a couple of pens to my outfit.

I pulled the spray out of my pocket, just to check again which way I needed to aim it.

"Where'd you find that?" asked Repro.

"I kind of borrowed it from a cop."

"Do you know how to use it?"

"Aim the spray and press," I said.

"Just make sure you're upwind," said Repro. "Blowback would be mighty painful."

"As soon as the door's opened, I'll use it on whoever gets in our way."

My voice may have sounded confident, but I was shaking with nerves. For the first time, I wasn't on the run from this woman and her associates – instead I was taking the fight right into her territory. I didn't know whether I'd find what I needed in her desk, but I hoped like anything that what we'd seen in the enhanced photograph was a copy of the Ormond Riddle, and I was willing to take the risk. I needed the edge over everyone else that was chasing this mystery.

"Are you ready?" I whispered to my companion.

Repro nodded.

"Here goes," I said, getting to my feet. I tidied myself up, combing back my hair and tucking the box of roses and the clipboard under my arm. I tried hard to look older, as if I did this every day for a living, strode boldly up to the front door and knocked.

Before long, footsteps approached the door, and it was yanked open by a guy that looked like a sumo wrestler. This was the guy that I'd seen with Oriana the night I was up the tree in their front yard, spying on them through the window. He was about as wide as he was tall — and that seemed like yards above me.

His eyes narrowed with suspicion. "What do you want, Buster?"

Buster. I remembered being called that the night in January when I was grabbed off the street. I was pretty sure he was also the one who threw me in the trunk.

Please don't recognize me!

I went straight into my script. "I have a box of roses to deliver to this address. For a," I stopped to look at my clipboard, "Ms. Oriana de la Force? Please sign here, sir."

I offered the box and the clipboard with a receipt for the guy to sign.

"Isn't it a little late for deliveries?" he asked with a snarl.

"Sorry, sir, you're the last stop of the day."

He frowned, grunted, and went to take the long box from me. In that moment I pulled the pepper spray out of my pocket and squeezed the vapor in his face. Payback time, I thought. He roared and staggered backwards, while I shoved the can back in my pocket.

Repro was behind me in a flash. "Hold your breath!" I shouted, "And cover your eyes as best you can!"

Together with Repro, I grabbed the reeling heavyweight, and we both pulled him out through the door, slamming it shut after him. He tumbled hard down the few front stairs.

I felt the spray stinging my eyes. I blinked. My eyes started streaming with tears. But I had other things to think about . . .

"You OK?" I asked Repro, who was sniffing beside me.

"I think so," he said.

Within seconds we'd raced up the stairs, running along the upstairs hallway, throwing doors open, until I found the room I was after — Oriana de la Force's study!

Across from her desk was a walk-in closet with stacks of dresses and shoes. On a shelf above the dresses, four red wigs on stands rested in a row, like severed heads. Beyond that was Oriana's lavish bedroom, done up in black and gold, and complete with a bulky chandelier. But I didn't have time to admire her interior decorating. We only had minutes before the guy downstairs recovered and tried to get back in.

"OK," said Repro, "what am I looking for?"

"Keep an eye on the window," I said, not pausing in my search through the papers on the top of the desk, "and tell me what the big guy is doing."

Repro did as I asked and peered out of the window but jumped back quickly. "The big guy looks like he's out cold — must have hit his head or something — but whatever you're looking for, you better find it fast," he said, "because the blue Mercedes is pulling up outside."

Feverishly, my fingers shaking from nerves because there was nothing on the desktop now, I started pulling the drawers out. From downstairs I could hear raised voices in the front garden. And only a few seconds later the front door must have opened, because I heard feet running through the downstairs hall. I cleared the second drawer. Nothing.

In the third drawer, I found a square silver case. Maybe she'd hidden the text of the riddle in here? My fingers were still shaking as I lifted it out. They slipped completely when I opened the lid and hundreds of little silver cachous bounced across the desk like tiny stones, before spilling to the floor. They shot out in all directions.

"Hurry, my boy!" Repro was bouncing up and down next to the window, alternately peering outside and turning to me.

I didn't need any extra urging — I was moving as fast as I could, straining to open the bottom drawer.

"Help me!" I yelled, as I heard footsteps starting to mount the staircase. "This drawer is locked!"

Repro pushed me out of the way, did something to the lock with a long, thin letter opener and yanked the drawer open. The footsteps thudded up to the top of the stairs. Any second now and they'd be in the study. Repro raced over to a heavy chest and started dragging it towards the other side of the room. I didn't have a chance to wonder what he was doing — I was sending papers flying as I searched through the pile in the bottom drawer, desperate to find the cream-colored paper Boges and I had seen in the photo. Behind me Repro was stacking furniture against the door. A bookcase was overturned, and dozens of books went flying all over the floor.

My desperate search turned up nothing remotely connected to the Ormond Riddle or the Ormond Angel. In the corridor, a couple of angry voices got louder as they thudded down the hallway towards the study.

Then, right at the bottom of the drawer, I spotted a paper folder. I flipped it open and saw a worn piece of thick parchment paper. I felt sure this was the cream-colored page we'd seen! Despite the sounds of Oriana de la Force's bodyguards bashing at the door, a thrill of excitement fizzed through my body. In old-fashioned, flowery writing, I read two powerful words . . .

"Ormond Riddle."

Beneath it, in the same trailing writing, were the lines of the Riddle!

The Riddle!

I'd been searching for this since January! I couldn't believe I was holding it in my hand! But how long was that going to last?

Somehow, we had to get away. No time to read anything now.

Already, the door was being pushed open in spite of Repro's mountain of furniture.

An arm appeared around the door, then a shoulder . . .

The door was opening!

Repro grunted and shoved another chair up to the pile in front of the slowly opening door. He turned around, pushing his weight up against the door. "Cal, get out the window," he ordered. "I can take these guys! Go, now!"

"I don't want to hear it!" I said. "They're going to be through that door in about five seconds and you're coming with me!"

I was halfway to the window, the precious Riddle folder in my hands, when the door burst open, throwing Repro to the floor.

One of the bodyguards hurtled through the air, coming straight for me.

He tackled me, and our eyes met. It was the guy with the teardrop tattoo! The guy I'd helped the night of the fire-bombing of the casino when he was being beaten up, back in January!

Kelvin!

In that moment of hazy recognition, he hesitated in surprise. His grip momentarily relaxed. I rolled clear of him sideways and scrambled up to the window, straddling the sill, with the Riddle folder clenched between my teeth . . .

I looked back to see Repro pounce on the teardrop tattoo guy. Even though he'd lied to me about the Singapore championships, Repro had him in what looked like a very strong hold.

"Get out!" he yelled, as he grappled with his opponent. "I can handle this!"

There was a terrible crash of furniture and the door to the study slammed shut again — but I knew it would only take a little while for someone else to get through all the piles of chairs and bookcases and stuff. I grabbed up the silver box and emptied the rest of the silver cachous onto the floor.

"Cal, what are you doing?! Get out!" Repro yelled again.

I looked back at him, uncertain whether I should go.

"Get out!"

Hoping that Repro was going to be OK to deal with whatever came crashing through the door, I threw myself out the window, leaping onto the tree outside.

A quick glance back showed Kelvin skidding on the tiny silver ball bearings that were scattered on the floor. Legs kicking uselessly, he crashed hard on his back.

Repro waved his hands at me, hurrying me away. I couldn't wait any longer. I took a huge breath, and on the count of three, I made a flying leap from the branches of the tree and hit the ground hard.

I was totally winded. I lay there for a second

while the night swirled around me. I felt like an elephant was sitting on me.

Finally the elephant got off my chest, and I rolled over onto all fours. I'd bruised myself against the can of pepper spray in my pocket, but somehow I'd kept hold of the folder with the Ormond Riddle in it. My fingers were sweaty around it.

I knew I had no time. I saw by the front stairs that the bulky body of the guy I'd sprayed earlier was just starting to stir — he must have tumbled down and bumped his head on a pillar outside.

Kelvin, or Oriana, would be charging into the garden after me any second. I didn't have time to worry about Repro. I hoped he could handle himself up there. I got to my feet and started running.

I had the Ormond Riddle in my grasp! It was only a matter of time before I understood the mystery of the Ormond Singularity and what it meant to my family.

9:02 pm

I didn't stop running, apart from slowing down to stow the Riddle folder in my bag, until I thought I was going to be sick from exhaustion. I wasn't sure where I was, and my whole body was throbbing like crazy, but I didn't care. *I've got it!* I thought. I've got the Ormond Riddle!

I couldn't wait to look at it and see if there was a connection that would explain Dad's drawings. But for now, I'd have to get out of town. Oriana would be after me with everything she had. I had stolen her precious Riddle. The city was way too small to hide me.

31 MARCH

276 days to go . . .

7:03 am

As the sun came up I found myself limping painfully along a narrow street after only a couple of hours of sleep under a small bridge. I was worried about how Repro had managed to escape the clutches of Oriana's bully boys. Right now I had no way of getting in touch with him to find out.

I decided to try my best and hold off on looking at the Riddle until I could call Boges and read over it with him. He was going to be so excited to hear that Repro and I had successfully snuck into Oriana's place and stolen the documents from her study. And, most of all, he'd be stoked that we finally had the actual text of the Riddle to work on!

My whole body was aching with exhaustion, but I felt great. This was one of the massive breaks that we'd been searching for that was finally going to get me some answers and help me out of this mess. This must have been how the famous archaeologists felt when they opened the tomb in the Valley of the Kings and, for the first time in thousands of years, light shone on Tutankhamen's solid gold sarcophagus.

What was in my backpack meant that I'd be able to make more sense of Dad's drawings. Had Oriana stolen the Riddle text from him? Or had she independently searched private collections to find it? With her contacts and position, that would be easier for her than for most people.

I also had to let Boges know that I was going to try and make my way to Mount Helicon where my old aviator great-uncle lived. I didn't know how I was going to get there, but I'd walk there if I had to.

11:48 am

I walked on and on, trying to get somewhere, but feeling pretty sure I was getting nowhere.

A wise Eastern saying that Boges used to quote started running through my head — that within every crisis was an opportunity — when a dusty pickup truck turned a corner and almost hit me with its bed.

As I jumped back onto the footpath, to let the pickup truck go past me, I saw a sudden opportunity. I made a split-second decision, grabbed the edge of the bed and launched myself up onto the back, rolling across some of the junk in there.

It was such a relief to be off my legs — they were both throbbing with pain — but I'd been crazy to think that the driver wouldn't notice me, no matter how reckless he was. I bumped along in the back of the bed for a couple of hundred yards until the truck slowed near a quiet spot along the road and pulled over.

The driver was getting out before I'd even had a chance to get to my feet. He was built like a bull, with broad shoulders, a thick neck and hair brushed back from a very angry, sunburned face.

"You! Get off my truck! What do you think you're doing?"

Too tired to argue, and too exhausted to beg, I threw my backpack onto the road and slowly clambered down.

"Let's take a look at what you've got in here," said the driver, picking up my backpack and rifling through it. "What do you think you're trying to do, jumping into the back of my vehicle?"

He was too big to argue with.

He pulled all my stuff out — clothes, the folder from Oriana's office, which he didn't bother to open — and dug right down to the bottom to find my bags of dried fruit and nuts, and the other tranquilizer syringes.

"What's this? Drugs?" He stared at me.

"They're veterinarian supplies," I said. "Look at the box. It says so."

He read the label, and then looked up at me again. "So what have you got these for?"

"I'm taking them to my great-uncle in the country," I said, without thinking. "He's got a farm at Mount Helicon. That's where I'm headed."

The guy gave me a hard look, which was interrupted by a cell phone ringing in the truck. He looked down at his watch and then quickly started shoving everything back into the backpack.

"Take it and get lost!" he said, as he threw the bag at me. It hit me so hard that I nearly fell over. I was just glad he didn't want to search my pockets or he would have found the pepper spray. That wouldn't have been so easy to explain.

He ran back to his truck and then sped off like a lunatic, sending gravel shooting up at my face.

12:23 pm

I could hardly walk now. Every step I took was like walking on hot coals. It wasn't just my feet hurting from the running, but the injuries on both of my legs that had been healing so well seemed inflamed and irritated by my jump from the tree at Oriana's.

Somehow, I had to get out of the city even if it meant walking all the way in agony.

Slowly, wincing with every step, I trudged along, hoping to find the main road west.

12:37 pm

I heard a vehicle approaching and swung around to see who it was driving up behind me on the road.

My heart sank. It was the pickup truck again. I didn't have the strength to deal with any more trouble. I couldn't run any farther.

The truck pulled right alongside me. I braced myself, not knowing what to expect.

"OK, get in," the guy called out through the open window.

I stared at him blankly.

"I've missed this morning's delivery already, and I told myself I'd pick you up if you were still here wandering along this road."

I hesitated. I wasn't sure what to do.

"What are you waiting for? You want a lift or not?" asked the driver, leaning across to unlock the door.

The thought of being able to sit back and rest up while being driven closer to my destination was way too much to pass up. I climbed in.

"Look, about before," he said, "bad morning, bad mood. There was no need for me to take it out on a kid . . . although you really shouldn't jump into the back of a moving vehicle."

"I know, sorry about that."

"The name's Lachlan Drysdale."

"Tom," I said, as we shook hands.

"So where exactly are you going, Tom?"

"My great-uncle's property," I said, probably a little carelessly, "in the Highlands. Mount Helicon."

"I can take you part of the way. You look pretty wrecked."

"I am," I agreed. "As far as you can would be great, thanks."

I rested my backpack against the window, and let my head fall on it.

2:52 pm

I woke up with a jolt, yelling and struggling, totally confused. Suddenly, I stopped, looking around with embarrassment, remembering where I was.

I was in the cab of Lachlan Drysdale's truck. The countryside was whipping past outside. I felt like a total idiot.

I looked over at him.

"You must have been having some nightmare," he said.

"Where are we?" I asked, struggling to sit up straight and look out at the landmarks around me. It seemed like we were well into the countryside now — thick bush grew along the roadside, the occasional homestead was set back from the road, and willow trees trailed their green ribbons along the river. It had been the rattling bridge crossing that had woken me up.

"You were out of it for ages. That must have been a powerful dream," laughed Lachlan. "You were kicking and thrashing around like the devil was after you!"

"It was full-on," I said, recalling the terrifying dream of moments ago. I'd been in the sea again with the sharks circling, when the Ormond Angel — who was now Winter — pulled me out of the water and threw me on the shore. But the white toy dog with blazing yellow eyes taunted me. It held the memory stick that he'd stolen from Jennifer Smith just out of my reach. I'd tried to grab it from him but suddenly the dog morphed into my double, and he was trying to kill me!

"Someone was after me," I explained lamely.

"Well I hope you got away, buddy," Lachlan joked. "So Tom, what's your story?"

"My story?" I said, worried for a second that he knew who I was. "Pretty simple really. I had to leave school and get a job. Family difficulties." That much at least was true. "But I thought I'd visit my old great-uncle first. He might know of some work."

Lachlan nodded as if he understood. "I'm hoping to start a new job, too. Big property in the riverland district. It's hard finding work in the country." He frowned and turned to me. "Wouldn't there be more work in the city?"

"I need to be outside. Can't stand that indoor work."

"I know what you mean," he nodded.

Country service station

4:55 pm

We stopped for a break and both bought pre-packaged sandwiches, chocolate and cans of drinks from the service station's cooler. I tried to give Lachlan some money for gas, but he waved it away. "I've got a job to go to. You keep your money, Tom."

I still had a hundred dollars, which I owed to Repro, hidden in my new shoes, but I didn't know how long that was going to last.

Repro . . . *I hope you got away OK.*

6:20 pm

After we'd been driving for another hour or so, I noticed that Lachlan seemed to be looking in the rearview mirror frequently. Something was worrying him.

"What is it?" I asked.

"Don't know if I'm being paranoid," he muttered, "but I reckon we're being followed."

I instantly felt sick, and my whole body tensed up.

He turned to me. "Who's after you, Tom?" he asked, seriously. Then he cracked up laughing. "You should see your face!"

I laughed along with him, realizing he was only joking around about someone being after me.

"I could be imagining it," he continued, "but there are not many of those huge off-road vehicles around, and this guy's been on my tail for quite a while now."

I turned around to see what he was talking about and sure enough, not far along the road behind us, was one of those huge SUVs, with a gleaming red and silver cab perched up on its monster, oversized wheels.

I slumped down further in the seat, trying to be inconspicuous. "How long has it been behind us?"

"Actually, I noticed them back when we left the city. They even stopped at the service station where we bought the sandwiches. It's not easy to miss a car like that! Or the driver! I got a look at him, and I've gotta tell you, I didn't like what I saw. He was even bigger and uglier than me! Looks like one of those Japanese wrestlers, and he had some other, weedier, character with him. Of course, they could always just be heading for the riverland district, too."

So the sumo wrestler and his mate, Kelvin, from Oriana's had tracked me down, and I knew they weren't heading for the riverland district.

"Sometimes you get a feeling for things," Lachlan continued. "I've got an instinct about people. I didn't like the look of them at all."

6:32 pm

We drove on a little way in silence, while Sumo and Kelvin stayed close behind us on the road.

"I must be completely paranoid," laughed Lachlan with a shake of his head, after looking in the rearview mirror once more. He glanced sideways at me and grinned. "Why would anyone be following us!"

I tried to laugh along with him, but I knew too well we had nothing but trouble ahead. I slumped even further down in my seat. This was no laughing matter — we were being followed. And they were following this pickup truck because they knew I was in it.

6:55 pm

"What's this guy trying to do?" Lachlan asked, glancing in the rearview mirror. I sneaked a look myself and snapped around again right away. The SUV had come up right behind us, almost touching the end of Lachlan's pickup, filling up the back window with its huge bull bar and fortified front end.

Then came a mighty bang and our pickup truck lurched forwards, causing us both to hit the dashboard! The monster truck was not only tailgating us, but bumping us along, rear-ending us.

"The guy's insane!" Lachlan yelled, leaning on his horn so that it blared loudly. "What's he trying to do? Knock us off the road?"

I said nothing, aware now that as well as trying to keep us straight on the road, Lachlan was staring hard at me.

"What are you doing? You're hiding!" he accused me. "Look at you, huddling down in the seat, trying not to be seen. You do know something about this, don't you?"

Another mighty rear-end bash struck and Lachlan battled with the steering wheel, struggling to keep the pickup truck straight on the road. Cars traveling in the opposite direction honked their horns in protest.

Just as he'd straightened the wheels, the SUV accelerated hard and bashed into the back of us again!

Lachlan yelled loudly. "You better tell me what's going on! This could get us both killed! If you know anything, start talking now!"

It was time to come clean.

"There are some people after me! They want something I've got, but it's not theirs. It's something my dad gave me, but he's dead now. It's a long story. I'm sorry," I pleaded, "I can't let them catch me! I need to stay alive so I can save the rest of my family!"

Another mighty crash from behind, and the pickup truck was lifted with only the two nearside wheels on the road. I clung onto the dashboard, terrified.

"We haven't got time for a long story!" he said, realizing the life-and-death seriousness of the situation. "I don't know why, but my instincts tell me you're all right. And if there's one thing I hate," Lachlan roared at the SUV in the rearview mirror, "it's bullies!"

7:19 pm

Again and again the mighty truck bashed into us, sending our smaller vehicle flying sideways and dangerously close to the oncoming traffic. If it was any busier on the other side of the road we both would have been written off in a head-on collision.

Another mighty bang from the truck behind us sent us swerving off the road, before Lachlan was able to gain control of the wildly swinging vehicle.

7:29 pm

He put his foot flat to the floor. "I'll get them off our tail! Watch this!"

Lachlan hit a switch under the dashboard and his truck lurched forward. I saw the speedometer increase from eighty miles per hour to 90, then 95, 100 . . .

Lachlan laughed with glee. "This reminds me of the last stock car rally I was in! We won, too!"

We were speeding, bouncing all over the road! Trees whizzed by. I clung on, hoping that

Lachlan was as good a driver as he thought he was. For a few moments, we pulled strongly away from the monster four-wheeler. I felt good, like we were going to make it! But this didn't last long. Soon the SUV's headlights had returned, and it was back in position, right on our tail.

Another huge crash, and our pickup went into a fishtail slide. Lachlan drove skillfully into the slide, correcting it.

"I think I'd better jump out," I said, thinking that this insane car chase couldn't go on any longer. "It's me they want. You don't have to die as well."

Speeding along like this could only end in death.

Lachlan glanced across at me. "Don't be crazy. As if I'd run out on you now."

He hunched over the steering wheel, bracing himself. "Just as well my rev-head mate hotted up this little pickup for me! We'll outrun them! Don't worry!"

But only a few minutes later, Lachlan frowned, his voice thin with tension. "I just can't shake them off! They're staying right on me!"

The speedometer was now clocking 110 miles per hour! I clung onto the seat while the roadside streamed past in a gray-green blur.

Suddenly there was an intersection ahead of us, and Lachlan swung the wheel to the right, hard and fast. The pickup truck screeched around the corner on its two right wheels with the entire left side up in the air. I would have crashed over on top of Lachlan except for the seatbelt that anchored me. Lachlan yahooed with triumph! "That got them! They didn't see that coming!"

The SUV continued racing through the intersection.

For the time being, we were rid of them.

8:22 pm

"We've lost 'em," Lachlan said suddenly. "Kid, you must be in some *massive* trouble!"

I leaned back in the seat and realized I'd been holding my breath. With a bit of luck, the SUV wouldn't find us again. I clutched my backpack. Inside was the most valuable document in the world. The text of the Ormond Riddle.

I unzipped my backpack and was just about to take out the Riddle and start looking at it when I heard Lachlan mutter.

"What is it?" I asked, but I already knew.

I turned and looked back, and sure enough there was the monster truck coming over a hill in the road some distance away.

Even while I watched, I could see it was gaining on us.

"We're calling the cops!" said Lachlan, throwing his cell phone to me as the truck moved into position behind the bed of his pickup.

I nearly said, "We can't!" But how could I? I was responsible for what was happening. If we were both run off the road and killed, it would all be my fault.

I started dialing while Lachlan desperately tried to control the vehicle. He swore again as his truck was bashed from behind and all four wheels left the road! For a few seconds, we were flying! I dropped the phone as we skidded, fishtailing wildly from side to side. I was thrown all over the cab until my seatbelt locked tight.

In a final effort to put distance between us and our attackers, Lachlan accelerated even more. By this stage, we were doing nearly 120 mph! At this speed, we were being thrown around the cab with every minor bump on the road. But it was no use! The huge monster easily kept up with us — in fact it was going faster! The driver was playing with us. He'd let us get ahead a little way just to give himself the run-up he needed for a final, vicious attack.

I leaned over trying to reach Lachlan's phone on the floor at my feet when the pickup was bashed forward, tipped up on its left-side wheels. Lachlan lost all control. With a sickening, gut-thumping lurch, we hit the slight embankment on the side of the road, hurtled over it, and continued crashing and bashing through the scrub. We both screamed as branches smashed the windshield, and the pickup was spun around and tipped all the way over onto its side where it slid, rolling over once completely to land upside down on a steep angle.

I grabbed my backpack, remembering the explosive caps I had in there, fearing injuries from them . . . if the crash didn't kill us.

I opened my eyes. I was hanging upside down in my seat, and I could hear the sound of running water. I screamed again as the pickup tipped and rolled once more, landing on its side in the shallow water of a creek, leaving me hanging sideways across the cab.

The impact of the seatbelt had winded me so badly that it felt like my breastbone had been pushed right through my chest and was now stuck to my spine.

But I knew I had to move fast. I took a big breath. I seemed to be in one piece, although my heart was racing like a machine gun. Then I became alarmed. There was no sign of my companion. He must have been thrown out on impact. As I scrambled to free myself, the pickup moved again, settling into the mud on the side of the creek.

Finally, I was able to undo my seatbelt and climb out of the cab and onto the upturned side of the pickup. I stumbled around to the driver's side, wading through the fast-running creek, to see what had happened to Lachlan.

He was pinned under the pickup, partly lying on the bank but with his head down, his face in the water! I grabbed him and pulled his shoulders as hard as I could. I was able to move him a little, but then I saw the problem. One of his arms was caught under the weight of the pickup — he was pinned and there was no way I could lift the truck off him. I grabbed his head and turned it sideways so that his face, at least, was out of the water.

He was unconscious, but he was breathing. As long as I held his head away from the water, he had a good chance of surviving. I couldn't see any injuries on him apart from some small cuts on his face and neck. But already I thought I could hear the crashing sound of the monster SUV as it followed our trail of destruction down to the creek.

"Wake up! Lachlan! Wake up!" I cried, holding his head with one hand, slapping his cheek with the other. If I could bring him around, he could keep his head up out of the water, and I could get away, promising to call the ambulance as I went. But he didn't open his eyes. I slapped him harder. "Come on, Lachlan! Wake up please!"

I could even hear their voices now as they yelled. In just a few moments, the sumo wrestler and his sidekick would be here. They would capture me and take the text of the Ormond Riddle that Repro and I had finally gotten hold of; they would find the drawings in my backpack. They would have everything. And I had no doubt that they would then dispose of me in a very permanent way.

I made another desperate attempt to bring Lachlan around, slapping his cheek hard, yelling his name.

I could hear them crashing through the bush, getting closer and closer. I knew I had two choices.

I could let go of Lachlan, grab my backpack with the precious Riddle and drawings and disappear into the bush. That way, I had a chance to save myself and the Ormond Riddle.

"Lachlan! Please wake up!"

But his head remained limp and heavy in my hands.

I could escape, but to do that I would have

to let go of Lachlan's head.

Without me holding his face away from the water, there was no question that Lachlan would drown.

Repro's face flashed across my mind. I could see him waving me through Oriana's window, telling me to go, telling me he'd be fine while he struggled with Kelvin. *But was he fine?*

I wouldn't leave anyone else behind.

I wouldn't let this man drown.

It was an impossible situation, but there really was only one choice. I had to stay and keep Lachlan alive.

Even if I used the pepper spray again, it would only be a matter of time before they overwhelmed me, and finally rid themselves of Callum Ormond, Psycho Kid.

I'd lost everything. Oriana's thugs were coming for me. They'd have the words to the Ormond Riddle again and they'd get my dad's drawings as well. They would discover the huge secret. Whatever the prize was, they would win it. The promise I'd made to Dad — that I'd continue his work until I cracked the secret — was broken now. I'd failed him, and I'd failed myself. I'd failed all of my family.

I looked up and glimpsed a figure on the ridge above me, and then I heard someone crashing and sliding down the slope towards me.

All I could do was crouch there and wait for them to come and get me . . .

03:32 01:47 05:03 MARCH LET THE COUNTDOWN BEGIN
10:45 RACE AGAINST TIME 06:48 07:12 05:51 RACE AG
RACE AGAINST TIME SEEK THE TRUTH ... CONSPIRACY
ONE SOMETHING IS SERIOUSLY MESSED UP HERE 05
05:06 06:07 MARCH WHO CAN CAN I TRUST? SEEK THE
MARCH 06:04 10:08 RACE AGAINST TIME 02:27 08:05
THE TRUTH 01:00 07:57 SOMETHING IS SERIOUSLY M
05:01 09:59 CONSPIRACY 365 13:00 RACE AGAINST TI
MARCH WHO CAN CAN I TRUST? 01:09 LET THE COUNT
MARCH HIDING SOMETHING? 03:32 01:47 05:03 MAR
COUNTDOWN BEGIN 09:06 10:33 11:45 RACE AGAINST
07:12 05:51 RACE AGAINST TIME RACE AGAINST TIME
TRUTH ... CONSPIRACY 365 TRUST NO ONE 06:07 SO
SERIOUSLY MESSED UP HERE 09:30 12:01 02:07 05:0
WHO CAN CAN I TRUST? SEEK THE TRUTH 13:05 MARCH
RACE AGAINST TIME 02:27 08:05 10:32 SEEK THE TR
SOME THING IS SERIOUSLY MESSED UP HERE 05:01 0
CONSPIRACY 365 13:00 RACE AGAINST TIME 04:25 10
CAN CAN I TRUST? 01:09 LET THE COUNTDOWN BEGIN
SOMETHING? 03:32 01:47 05:03 MARCH LET THE COU
09:06 10:33 11:45 RACE AGAINST TIME 06:48 07:12 0
AGAINST TIME RACE AGAINST TIME SEEK THE TRUTH
365 TRUST NO ONE SOMETHING IS 06:07 SERIOUSLY
HERE 09:30 12:01 03:07 05:06 06:07 MARCH WHO CAN
SEEK THE TRUTH 13:05 MARCH 06:04 10:08 RACE AG
02:27 08:05 10:32 SEEK THE TRUTH 01:00 07:57 SOM
SERIOUSLY MESSED UP HERE 05:01 09:59 CONSPIRA
RACE AGAINST TIME 04:25 10:17 MARCH WHO CAN CA
LET THE COUNTDOWN BEGIN MARCH HIDING SOMET
01:47 05:03 MARCH LET THE COUNTDOWN BEGIN 09
RACE AGAINST TIME 06:48 07:12 05:51 RACE AGAINS
AGAINST TIME SEEK THE TRUTH ... CONSPIRACY 36
SOME THING IS 06:07 SERIOUSLY MESSED UP HERE
05:07 05:06 06:07 MARCH WHO CAN CAN I TRUST? SE